# Fauna

David Hartley

First published September 2021 by Fly on the Wall Press

Published in the UK by Fly on the Wall Press

56 High Lea Rd

New Mills

Derbyshire

SK22 3DP

www.flyonthewallpress.co.uk

Copyright Dr. David Hartley © 2021

ISBN: 9781913211608

Fly on the Wall Press is committed to the sustainable printing and shipping of their books.

This collection is dedicated to all the staff and volunteers at the Manchester and Salford RSPCA, and to all those people who have stepped out of their human heads to do something genuinely nice for an animal, large or small.

# Acknowledgements

Broadcast of the Foxes was first published in *Structo Magazine*
Shooting an Elephant first appeared in *Ambit Magazine*
A Place to Dump Guinea Pigs was performed at the
'Gods and Monsters' event at Liar's League, London
Flock first appeared in the 'Humanagerie' anthology with
Eibonvale Press
Come and See the Whale first appeared in *The Cabinet of Heed*
Betamorphosis was first published in *The Shadow Booth*
Hutched first appeared in *The City Fox* and was reprinted in
*Foxhole Magazine*
A Time Before Horses was first published in *Shooter Literary*
*Magazine*
A Panda Appeared in Our Street was first published
on *STORGY.com*
The Bycatch was published in *BFS Horizons*

# Contents

# Broadcast of the Foxes

The fox has made a nest in your satellite dish and feasts on your children's fingers. You can't get a good signal. You can't watch your favourite programmes. You can't keep up with the news.

The fox, still hungry, lifts his mighty wings, spreads his crackling feathers through a ripple of red and green, then splits himself into a million tiny pieces, a firework of fur. Scattered, he seeps through the mortar of your house, seeks pathways in cracks in the brickwork, finds damp to bathe in and mould to lick.

But when he finds a rip in the wallpaper he peers through and watches you. He watches you think. He watches your thoughts. He watches you cross the room. He watches you pick up the phone. He watches you shout into the receiver.

"999," you shout. "999. I need the newspapers. 999. Tell the newspapers."

The phone is dead. The fox chewed through the wire three days ago.

He has eaten your children's fingers.

Upstairs, your children are crying.

Your signal is intermittent.

You cannot watch Great British Bake-Off.

"999," you shout, "999."

There is no-one there to hear you.

The sun slips away as if scared. Twilight creeps out and reclaims the world. The fox rises from your bricks and reforms. He is still hungry.

He leaves one eye behind to keep watch and stalks the streets for flesh. He is nightflame. Every step of his paw is another pothole, every swish of his paintbrush tail leaves a tag across shutters and walls. His stare beheads flowers, his bark topples bins, his claws awaken every sleeper to sweats and shivers.

He is your every complaint, your every inconvenience. He is your shame and your shadow. He is your simmering rage.

You've stayed up late. You've given up with the phone, no answer. You've shut out the wails of the children and you've sat down to write a letter.

Your anger swirls. You grip the pen like a talisman. You carve the words so deep into the paper they will never escape.

The fox hears your scritching, your scratching. He hears every letter you etch. The message amuses him. He forgets his empty belly.

He turns tail, heads for home.

*999, you write, 999. Police? I need the newspapers. No-one will help me. No-one cares about me. 999. I need the newspapers. Get me the newspapers.*

His teeth shine in the moonlight.

Your children pick at their wounds and sob.

Your signal is weak.

You've missed Line of Duty.

*999, you write, 9999999999999.*

You post the letter through your own letterbox, backwards. It lands upon the soggy pile on your doorstep.

It will never be read.


The fox has found a vixen. He has brought her to your home and they copulate in your satellite dish. They suck the last bits of flesh off the bones of your children's fingers.

They watch you while you sleep. They snigger every time you squirm.

The fox likes you. The fox finds you amusing and he feels sorry for you. You made tasty children and he promises not to eat too much more of them. A few toes perhaps, maybe an eyeball. And the vixen might need an arm to chew on, but just one.

He likes you. He will tip the balance in your favour. He will keep you going for as long as he can. He will not make it easy for the others.

The weather is on shuffle. It burns hot one hour, spits hail the next. It rages through a storm and then settles to stillness. Each shift adjusts like a valve in your brain and you pop awake and fume your way back to half-sleep.

You didn't see the forecast. You don't know if this was predicted. You missed the news.

The fox and vixen don't feel weather. Nothing disturbs their hunger, nor their licking of the bones. Nothing stops their barks and giggles, nothing distracts, nothing shames.

The fox knows he nearly has you. The fox knows the time draws close.

You wake and illuminate your face with your phone. You open metro.co.uk. You find a comments box and press for the pop-up of the keyboard.

999, you type, 999. I need yous to help. I have a story. bring ur newspaper 2 me. 34 albion street. plz come now. police wont help. 999. i need the newspapers. plz help.

The fox impregnates the vixen.

Your children bleed over the bedsheets and weep themselves to sleep.

There is no signal.

The comment fails to post.

You watch the buffer circle spin and spin until the phone blinks out and dies.


The day breaks. The fox feels the morning crack awake like a sudden whip and he knows it is time. He knows the day has arrived.

Phone, letter, internet. Your options are gone. There is nothing left. There is one thing left. The fox watches the tiny muscles of your face and reads your thoughts. They are as slow as lazy clouds, but clear.

There is nothing left, there is one thing left. You stare out of the window. The day is here, the moment has come.

The vixen slips through the floorboards. She spirits along woodgrain and finds your children's bedroom. It stinks of gangrene, but she doesn't mind. She will tend to them, look after them, she will resist the hunger in her belly.

9

She likes your children, she means them no harm.

You stare out of windows. You stare out of every window. You move from room to room, from window to window. The fox follows, your shadow, your ghost. He blows and blows at the walls, wills them to fall, urges you to make the move, screams at you to go. You stare out of windows. It looks cold outside.

The fox leaps and lands on your back. He wraps his tail around your neck like a scarf and breathes hot breath across your cheeks. His heart thumps against the back of your head and the warmth washes through you like steam. You break out into a sweat.

You open the window. You put a hand out and feel the air. It wants you, you think. It wants to take you out.


You climb out of the window and emerge onto the street. The fox unravels and leaps to the roof, his tail a newborn bonfire. He leaps from spot to spot like CCTV, every image showing you stride down your street.

You look at your neighbourhood. No-one around. No-one out to play. Mess everywhere. The sky is a sickening red, the clouds look ready for war. Everything is silent, nothing moves, everything waits. Except you.

On you march, feet slicing open on bits of broken glass. You reach the main road. You look left, you look right. No cars, no life.

Except one thing. A fox. Mangy-looking. Sitting on top of traffic light stuck on red. Watching you. Grinning, you think.

You take a deep breath and hold it. Every hair on the fox's body rises. His tail stops. His claws flex. He is ready.

He is your every grievance. your every irritation, your simmering rage. You are standing at the end of your street at the end of your time, naked, freezing, sweating and angry. You breathe out.

"999," you shout. "999 I need the newspapers. Bring the newspapers. I need to tell my story. I need help. 999! Tell the newspapers."

Your fox barks and receives a thousand barks in echo.

The foxes have heard your broadcast.

Your signal was strong.

"999," you whisper.

The foxes are coming. The hunt is on.

# Shooting an Elephant

He strode in, the first customer of the day, an angular man with sleepless eyes. He flicked out his card from a magicked nowhere and slapped it into place on the desk.

"Elephant," he said.

"Certainly sir. Please take a seat in the waiting room."

I processed the payment. It cleared without problem so I clicked it straight through to the troupe. I hoped they were fully stretched and limber. The gentleman didn't strike me as the patient type.

On my monitor the Arena waited, blank and serene. A few moments of stillness passed then the troupe swarmed in, lithe bodies in grey Lycra. They chalked up and I set the atmos to Savannah. Helen spoke a few words to the group, strode to the camera and held up two hands, fingers splayed. I moved out from behind the desk and approached the gentleman. He was already deep into mime and didn't look up when I spoke.

"There'll be a ten-minute wait, sir," I said. "You're first in today and we like to allow time for the atmos to settle. Can I get you a drink?"

He grunted and shook his head. I nodded and left him alone.

Back at the desk, I swiped the waiting room onto the monitor. The gentleman's mime was complex and precise. He was stooped over a case of some kind and his rifle was in sections. He picked up and inspected each part then slotted them together and faked the weight of it across both hands. He frowned and took it apart again. For a long while he cleaned the barrel, a frantic hand buffing thin air, then he made minute adjustments to what I assumed was the dial for the scope. He slotted it back together, clicked his tongue as every piece found its place. He snapped the magazine in with a pop of his lips and flicked the safety catch. I couldn't tell if he'd switched it on or off.

He closed the case and propped it against the wall. He laid the gun across his lap and waited, hands hovering just above his legs. I checked in on the troupe. They were ready. Helen swung from the front of the face, her body curled into a very convincing trunk.

The gentleman crouched as he waited for the Arena doors to open. His pointy elbows and knees made him look like a cricket. He had one thumb pressed upon his shoulder where the strap of the rifle lay. His other hand pressed invisible binoculars against his chest.

I put him on all the monitors as he made his way inside, including the online live stream. The gentleman stalked forward and hid behind a shimmering bush. He put the binoculars to his eyes and peered across the Arena. The elephant was grazing only a couple of hundred metres away.

I switched angles. The troupe's beast was as magnificent as ever. Sixteen of the men in four groups made up the legs, belts locked. They gripped the ankles of the youngsters above them who curved back and interlaced to form the width and bulk of the body. At the rear, Lucia's gentle arm flopped loose to make a tail.

Darren, Geri and José made up the head. José in the middle, Darren and Geri either side, their outer arms hidden in the controls of the Lycra earflaps. José was braced by an army of hands so that he in turn could hold onto Helen. She swung upside-down in full trunk mode. She bent herself around a bundle of straw and passed it up to — who was that? I changed the angle — Carla, one of our newest recruits. Carla did an exemplary job of pulsing the bundle to let the elephant chew before making it all disappear inside. I allowed myself a small smile. Our service was second to none.

I changed the angle and brought the gentleman back into view. He crept out from behind the shrub and shifted his shoulder to swing off the rifle. He advanced on the elephant, watched his step for our virtual twigs. He reached the edge of a rocky outcrop and dropped to one knee. He clicked his tongue as he loaded a bullet into the chamber. José gave a quick grunt and the elephant's head lifted and turned. Geri raised an ear. José huffed.

The gentleman stayed very still and waited. The elephant took a few tentative steps away then Helen swung down and the scour for food resumed. The gentleman sidestepped behind the rocks and lay down. It was a good position.

He flattened himself and brought his hands up. His shoulder kinked back as the stock found its place. I zoomed in. He closed one eye and peered down the scope. His finger curled against the trigger.

I flicked to an angle behind and framed the troupe in the distance. The gentleman fired and shouted the bang. The troupe flinched as the shot hit. Tomas was the closest and he was quick to let the red ribbon spurt from the back of the elephant's head. It sprang out and left a twisting trail. José bellowed his best roar and the elephant bolted.

The gentleman fired off another shot and hit the left flank then leapt off the outcrop and sprinted across the Arena in pursuit. The elephant made good progress but stumbled as the first wound took hold in the brain. It twisted back to try and rid itself of the trail of ribbon spooling from its rump. The gentleman lifted the rifle and fired then tugged on the reload and fired again. The two bullets found their marks in the face and José was smeared in bursts of red. The troupe slumped and José gave a muffled cry. The gentleman strode to the dying beast and emptied the magazine into its heart.

He posed for the picture but didn't smile. The Arena flashed when I pressed the icon and the image filled my monitor seconds later. I ported it onto the keyrings and fridge magnets and waited for the gentleman to emerge. As soon as the Arena doors opened he burst out, marched straight to the desk and slapped down his card.

"Again," he said.

It was the first time in my career I had ever hesitated. I cancelled off the photographs and cleared my throat.

"Elephant?" I asked and he nodded. He would not make eye contact with me.

I processed the payment. It cleared.

"Certainly sir. Take a seat."

"Ten minutes," he said, as he thumped away.

Five minutes later Mr and Mrs Booth arrived.

"Morning Sami," they said, almost in unison.

"Good morning Mr and Mrs Booth."

"Today's the day," said Mrs Booth.

Mr Booth put an arm around her shoulders and grinned. He lifted his card and rapped it against the desk.

"Giraffe, Sami. The best you have." He winked and Mrs Booth giggled. They had been saving up for this for some time.

"Certainly Mr and Mrs Booth," I said. I did not allow my smile to falter. "There will be a short wait."

They peered into the waiting room. "Oh no bother. We've got plenty of time," said Mrs Booth.

"You can take the payment now Sami."

I processed the money. "Thank you. Take a seat. I'll bring through some tea."

"You're a good'n."

They bustled into the waiting room and sat opposite the gentleman. Mrs Booth tried her hardest to catch his eye so she could smile her way into a conversation. The gentleman was resolute in his denial that anything else existed. He pointed his right hand into a revolver shape and twisted it to let the chamber fall loose. He clinked in the bullets with his left thumb then snapped the chamber back in and spun it. He made the noise like a purring cat and stuffed his fingers into a holster at his hip.

Mr and Mrs Booth joined me in reception as the gentleman made his way inside for the second hunt.

"Curious chap," said Mr Booth. "What's that he's shooting with? Pistols?"

"Revolvers I believe. Two of them." Both the gentlemen's hands were pointed into gun shapes, thumbs cocked as hammers.

"Funny things to hunt an elephant with," said Mrs Booth.

Mr Booth leaned closer to the screens. "What on earth is he doing?"

The gentleman did not bother taking cover this time. He strode straight towards the troupe, hands at his sides like a cowboy. The troupe tottered, not quite sure how to react. They couldn't pretend they hadn't seen him. Lucia whipped the tail, Darren and Geri raised the ears. The leg-men stood firm.

The gentleman stopped and fired into the air. His bang was loud and his mouth flapped as he sounded off the echoes too. I saw a frown flicker across José's face. He whispered something to Geri and she passed it through the whole elephant like a twitch. Helen stiffened as José lifted her and trumpeted.

The gentleman lowered his hand back to his hip and stood his ground.

"What's his game?" chuckled Mr Booth. Mrs Booth gripped her husband's arm. I switched the angle for a wider view.

The gentleman shouted: *hey, hey, hey!* The elephant tottered, José huffed. Darren and Geri raised the ears to full height and the head lowered. The four men of the front left leg jumped and made the elephant stomp.

The gentleman didn't flinch. The elephant charged.

He waited and waited and waited, then lifted his hands and cracked off round after round, straight into the elephant's head. At the last moment, he leapt and rolled away. The troupe skidded and crashed to the floor, chest first. There was half a moment when I thought they were going to give it all up; I could see irritation on their faces and Carla looked as if she had taken quite a knock to the shoulder. But they stayed together. José made all the right agonised sounds. Gouts of ribbon spouted from the holes in the head and streamed across a limp Helen. The body rose and fell with laboured breaths.

"Christ almighty," whispered Mr Booth.

Without a care in the world, the gentleman stripped bullets from a bandolier and reloaded both his hands. He walked up to the troupe and peered into a few faces. Then he clambered onto the elephant's back and banged the twelve rounds directly into the base of the skull. I hit the alarm and the Arena flooded red.

"You can't do that," said Mrs Booth. "You just can't do that, Sami." Her worried eyes met mine. I pressed for the intercom.

"I'm sorry sir," I said, a quiver in my voice. "No climbing. Please return to reception. Your session is now void."

He stared into the camera, leapt off the complaining troupe and set off for the door. The elephant dissipated as sore acrobats broke off and rubbed bruises.

"No respect," tutted Mr Booth. "No goddamn respect." He put his arm around Mrs Booth whose face looked shrunken.

I took a deep breath and opened the Arena doors. The gentleman burst out and slammed his card onto the desk.

"Again," he said.

Mr Booth tutted.

"I'm afraid we have other customers waiting and-"

"Again."

I stood my ground. "Mr and Mrs Booth are next sir-"

The gentleman raised his gun-hand and pointed it at Mr Booth's head. Mrs Booth screamed. Mr Booth gave a nervous laugh and stepped back.

"Ok, ok," he said, "we're happy to wait Sami. Let the man have his fun."

The gentleman lowered his hand but kept the gun shape. "Again," he said.

I pressed my lips together and processed the payment. It cleared. The gun hand disappeared and the gentleman pushed past Mr and Mrs Booth to resume his seat in the waiting room. I clicked it through to the troupe and heard the echo of Helen's swear as she received it.


This time there was no mime. The three of us watched him carefully on my monitor, the Booths besieged behind my desk. This would be the gentleman's last session. I was determined. I was planning some sort of statement on behalf of the troupe and had a call to the local security on standby.

The gentleman was sitting very still. No fixing up of a weapon, no movement of any kind. I looked at each part of his scrawny body. Did he have an invisible machete strapped to his back? A dagger on his calf? Some kind of blowpipe on a string around his neck? We checked in on Helen. The elephant was reformed and grazing at the far end of the Arena, the furthest point from the door. I wondered what their play was.

I let the gentleman sweat for a little while longer. The time stretched to fifteen minutes before he began to tap his foot.

"Better let him in," muttered Mr Booth.

"The Arena is ready," I said through the intercom.

The gentleman stood and his hand gripped around the handle of a case. From the straightness of his arm and the stiffness in his shoulder, it seemed to be quite heavy and cumbersome. He hobbled past us and waited by the door. I opened it and he bustled through.


"I don't like this," said Mrs Booth.

The gentleman huffed his way to the outcrop. He stopped twice to rest his arm and flex his carrying hand. The troupe stayed well away but kept the elephant on the move. It strode around the edge of the Arena. This one looked older than the previous two.

The gentleman laid his case across the rocks and opened it. He lifted out a large object using both hands and put it on the floor. He closed the case, set it aside then fiddled for a while with his weapon.

"What is it?" whispered Mr Booth. "Is this allowed?"

"I don't know." I eyed the call for security, almost pressed it.

The gentlemen curled his hand into a scope and peered through it. He moved his free hand to the end and twisted. I changed the angle to the camera nearest the elephant to get a better impression of the troupe's point of view. They would have to get closer if they wanted to act this one out with any accuracy. I could see the same thoughts pass across José and Helen's faces. The elephant soon began to amble away from the edge to a more open space. I checked the live stream. There were thousands of people watching.

The gentleman lowered his scope and stashed it away. He stood for a while with his hands on his hips and waited for the slow advance of the elephant of acrobats. When there was a clear line of sight, he picked up the weapon and lifted it onto his shoulder.

He lowered to one knee and leaned his head in. One eye closed as the other hovered behind a viewfinder.

"Bazooka," said Mr Booth. I called security.

The gentleman fired and leapt away. He shouted a loud boom and a violent swoosh as the rocket cut open the air, and then jumped and threw his arms wide as the explosion blew from his cheeks.

The troupe flung apart. Ribbon sprang and whipped, bodies hurtled high and limbs flailed. The leg-men crumpled and sprawled, José and Darren fell inwards while Geri sprung out head-first and crashed against the wall. Helen folded hard into the ground and shriveled up just as a splatter of acrobats came thudding to the floor. The ribbon twirled and settled. For a sickening moment there was nothing. Then Carla started to scream.

My finger shook as I cancelled the live stream. Mrs Booth whimpered. Carla's femur was sticking out of her knee joint. I could see three other acrobats unconscious, including Geri. Heads began to rise to look at Carla, agony breaking on their faces as they too discovered wounds and fractures. The gentleman strode over to the edge of the chaos and watched it. He turned and crouched, thumbs up but no smile.

"Sick bastard wants a picture," said Mr Booth. I did not give him the satisfaction.

I pressed for the medics and cleared out the atmos. The Arena faded to blankness as all the outcrops, bushes and trees shimmered out. The gentleman took a last look at the carnage and began to walk calmly back to the exit. Security were still three minutes away, the medics ten.

"Go through to the office," I said to the Booths, "I'll do what I can."

The Booths did as they were told. I grabbed the first aid kit - a beautiful connection between the flesh of my palm and the mottled green plastic of the handle - and marched to the Arena door.

I broke into a run as I entered. Carla's screams filled the hall, a dead sound without atmos, primal and hollow, almost pure. For a moment I smelt the heat of the Savannah, the choke of dust, a raw prickle on drying lips, a sticky glaze of sweat at my hairline, but it soon faded into the cool silver-grey of air-con and strip lights.

I looked at the gentleman. He was strolling towards me, mimes all gone, lost in a happy somewhere. As we drew close he looked me hard in the eye. He halted me. Snared me.

He placed his fist to the side of his head and formed a gun with his other hand. He put the gun to his temple, thumb-cocked, and fired.

"Pow," he said.

He released his fist and a stream of ribbon fluttered out. It was a poor mime. The tangled ribbon clumped to the floor. I picked it up and stuffed it in my pocket. It was my job to keep everything clean. It was my job to keep everything correct. Carla screamed and screamed. The man carried on walking and did not look back.

# A Place to Dump Guinea Pigs

Heard his 'eartbeat before I saw him and yeah, I was excited, but I was also like; ay up, a live one. What fun 'n games we got now? Immortal? 'ero? Or just someone badly lost?

It had been a while. The longest while. I'd figured 'em all dead; that I'd long taken my last boat-load over. But why would I still be here? So maybe they're all immortal now - one of Zeus' millennial whims, some bizarre pact between him and a wronged lover or summat. But I'd have heard somethin'. Hades would've been over in a flash to sort that shit out.

Maybes there's another way over my river, or under it, or around it that I don't know about, Or perhaps they've all buggered off to Elysium. I even wondered if there was anyone left over t'other side; tempted more than once to row over and have a look. But, nah; if I was supposed to know, I'd know, and I've been stuck here thousands o' years, what's a few more? I ain't interested in nowhere else to live.

Had some hangers-on to keep me company. The chancers who didn't have enough coin first time 'round and were paying their 100-year penance. Some of 'em were alright as well, we had a laugh. But I punted 'em over one by one when their long-awaited time came, until there was no-one left but little old me.

And then this guy comes. This bloke. With his heartbeat and his bag full of guinea pigs.


How to describe 'im? Well clothing's changed. A lot neater, tighter, and much more colourful. He weren't wearing a cloak, but his top bit were like a smaller cloak just for his top half, and it had a hood, which he had up. And the top had a big number on't back. A zero, and an eight. I didn't understand; was he the eighth of somethin'? If so, I hadn't seen t'other seven. And his trousers were dark blue, and on his feet he had these half-boots which were the brightest white. Hair on his face, but short and patchy. His belly and neck were fat as, but rest of him looked alright. Except 'is eyes. He had gloom in 'is eyes. Could never quite look directly at me.

And he has this bag, this red bag. Made of really thin material, and pulled tight at the top with a drawstring. And whatever was inside was wriggling an' whining an' squealing and had its own pattern of tiny heartbeats. Certainly the strangest thing that's ever come to shores of the Styx, an' I've seen some weird shite in my time.

So I says, Greetings.

And he says; How much is it for 'alf-way across?

And I says; I don't go 'alf-way, I go all't way. There's no 'alf-way.

And he says; Well I don't wanna go all't way, I wanna go 'alf-way.

And I says; It's all way or nothin' fella.

And he says; What difference does it make all way or 'alf way?

Part of me wanted to keep arguin' toss with him cus I definitely don't go 'alf-way, but he was the first bloke I'd seen for a couple of thousand year and I hadn't seen any coin for that long either.

So I says; How much you got?

And he checked and said; Twenty-eight quid.

He puts the stuff in my hand. I don't know 'quid'. I figured it some sorta new currency what must of developed. Bits of coloured paper and a few weird-looking coins of different shapes, sizes an' metals.

I said; I only do silver obols, and he pointed at some of the coins and said; That's silver, and these ones 'ere are gold, and that bit of paper is worth twenty of them golds, and in't that enough?

I figured I maybe should just take what I can get these days. So I says; Aye, alright, I'll fetch me boat.

And he says; Cheers mate, appreciate it.

And I says; You sure you only want to go 'alf-way?

And he says; Aye, 'alf-way.

And I says; What's in't bag?

And he says; Never mind about that.

So I gets me smallest boat and we head out. And I must admit, it feels reet good to be back on't river again, reet nice to stretch out the ol' rowin' bones. But the man doesn't relax. He says; Just take me to the deepest bit.

And I looks at him and I see he's got hold of some little rocks and he's opened't bag and he's puttin' the rocks in there. And every time one of them rocks hits whatever's inside, I can hear 'em whining louder, an' squealing, an' then making this weird little rumbling noise.

And I don't know; I'm not 'appy about this. I've not got good feelin'. I mean doesn't he know the etiquette? Doesn't he know that you've gotta treat the ferryman with the utmost respect? That no-one; not the dead, not the living, not the trumped-up heroes, not even't Gods can disrespect the ferryman. Without me, no-one gets nowhere. Without me, everyone stays the wrong side of the Styx. Everyone gets trapped between this life and't next.

So, I stop rowing, sit down and he says; Is this it?

And I say; No this in't it. I says; I ain't going any further 'til you tell me what's in that bag.

And he says; You don't need to know.

And I says; Yes, I do need to know. Unless you wanta spend the rest of your every breaths here in this boat, on this river, with me, I do need to know.

And he says; Well I'll just row myself.

And I says; The Styx won't let you do that. (Which is bullshit, but it sounds good.)

And he stops for a bit. His face goes all red and his gloomy eyes bulge. Then he huffs an' opens the bag wider.

He says; They're guinea pigs.

And I says; They're what?

He says; Guinea pigs. Animals. Little rodents.

I look inside and there they are. Three fat little furry blobs, all pressed up against each other. One's white, one's brown and another smaller one is a patchwork of both colours. One of the little fellas lifts its head and I can see a tiny nose sniffing the air, two black little eyes and funny flappy ears on the sides of its 'ead. They almost don't look real. Like someone's drawed 'em on parchment and they've come to life

25

somehow.

So I says; What you doin' with them?

And he says; I'm getting rid.

I says; Why?

And he says; They're a pain in the arse, that's why.

And I sit back down. I'm hit with this horrible wave of sadness.
Like the Styx itself has just reached up and swallowed me. I ain't never
seen a guinea pig before, ain't never 'eard of 'em before, but it's clear
that this is not right at all. This fella is planning on dumping them little
fellas overboard and the poor buggers won't have a fightin' chance in all
creation. I can't imagine those tiny things ever doing any hurt to anyone,
let alone this man with his fat neck.

You can't do that, I says.

Do what I want, he says. They're my guinea pigs.

So I says; Well why can't you just give 'em to someone else?

But he says; Tried that, no-one wants the bloody things. Fact is,
right – and he starts counting this off on his fingers – they're too bloody
expensive, too bloody dirty, too demanding, and they keep getting sick
all the time. And now they're multiplying. They've got to go. Nothing
else for it. Should never have bothered with 'em in't first place.

But why'd you get them in the first place, then?

Got 'em for the kids, but they're not interested no more, and
youngest is allergic. Look I don't wanna have to do this, but got no other
choice.

And I'm gripping side of the boat now, proper hard, because of
course he had other choices, of course he could've done more, of course
it didn't have to come to this. I don't want be any part of it, so I says so,
I tells him, I say; I'm not going to let you do that.

And he stands up. Yes you are mate, he says. I've paid you good
money for you to do your job. That's all you're here for; to do the rowing. So don't give me no grief, pick up your fuckin' oars, take me to the
deepest bit, then take me back. That's it. That's your job. I'll let you do
what you do, and you let me do what I've got to do. Alright?

And that sadness hits me again. The fight goes out of me. He's
right. He's paid for my services and that's what I'm bound, by ancient
laws, to do. So I pick up the oars, let him sit back down, and I set to the

rowin' again.


Fact is, I don't know where the deepest bit of the Styx is. I don't know nuffin' about anything under the surface. In all my years I've never had cause to go down, and no-one's ever come here to measure it. So I takes the boat around in a couple of wide circles and stop when I feel like stopping. It's dark out here, he can't tell.

Alright then, I says.

And he says nothing now. He pulls the string tight as it'll go and lowers the bag to the surface. It bobs there for a second, and I listen hard at those tiny heartbeats as they thump faster, like they know summat bad is coming. And then Styx takes them into her darkness, and the bag disappears.

The fella's long since stopped watching. He looks shrunken now, like by losing the bag he's somehow lost 'alf himself too. He radiates shame. You can see it blazing off him like rolls of fire. This ain't making him happy. I doubt there's anything that actually makes him happy.

Right then, he says.

It's my turn to say nothing. Just do what I'm here to do. I row.


He steps ashore and takes one deep breath; in and out. He turns to me.

Listen, he says. Thanks for that, alright? Sorry I had to get a bit... y'know.

He puts his hand out and I copy him. He takes my hand in his an' squeezes it just a little too hard.

Which way's out?

I point him up the slope and he strides away.


I sit for a while, my toes in the water, thinking it all through. The thing is, there's something he doesn't know about the Styx. Something him and his lot must've long forgot. It ain't like a normal river. Its waters are just as dead as everything else around 'ere. But it's still a living

27

thing too, in a way. It's the soul of a river, 'alf-way between the two, bit like myself. So you can chuck stuff in it, weight it down, but that don't mean it makes them things dead. The Styx'll just hold them. Freeze them in time. So likely those guinea pigs are still alive down there, still wriggling over each other, pushing at them rocks.

And I'm having strange thoughts. I'm thinking, I could just go on in there and fetch 'em out. Nothin' stopping me. No rules about it. No-one around to see.

So that's exactly what I do. Get back in the boat, row to the spot and lower myself in. I can feel the Styx askin' me a million questions, wondering what in the ages is happening, but I ignore her as only I know how, and put my head under.

It's as clear as day beneath the surface for my sharp eyes and it don't take long to find t'bag. And I'm right, the fellas are still wriggling, hearts still poppin'. And for't first time in a long time I feel important. I feel what it really feels like to be important. Not just needed, not essential, but significant. I push myself down to the bag and take it in both hands.


Back on my shore, the guinea pigs are trotting around in the little space I've made, shaking themselves dry, sniffing the air with their funny snouts, chattering away to each other in their ancient language. I must admit to being mesmerised. Besotted. Big stupid grin on my face.

Everything they do is another tiny delight. Wiping their faces with their front feet. Squaring up to each other. Their shrill little calls; wheek wheek wheek. The littlest one keeps sneezing, then he runs about a bit doing all these daft little skips.

I says to them; Hey, guinea pigs, if you want to get across you have to pay me one silver obol each.

Wheek, wheek they say, so I'm like; Tut tut, you'll have to stay here wi' me for't next hundred years.

But they seem fine about that to me. So I'll let them stay. Maybe even longer if I can swing it. Us abandoned ones are best stickin' together.

And while I'm sitting there thinking of some good names to call 'em, my thoughts drift back to the man. I wonder if he's realised yet, that I took him to t'other shore. I wonder if he's stumbled across Cerberus, if the hound still lives. Perhaps he's made it all the way to the throne of Hades. The bloke's heart still beats of course so he'll not be allowed to stay down here forever. But Hades can have him for a bit. New plaything for our mighty Lord. And when he gets bored of the man, well it's his problem then in't it? He'll find somewhere else for him. Somewhere quiet. Somewhere cold. Somewhere dark.

I'll call 'em Hera, Athena and Hebe. I'm sure the ladies won't mind.

# Flock

Imagine it was you.

You could have been doing something profound, like walking along the canal-side contemplating divorce, or attending the funeral of your best friend's child. Or walking free from a three-year jail sentence, or celebrating the patent of your invention with a picnic for one in the park.

But perhaps you were doing something more mundane. Hanging out the washing. Bringing in the bins. Walking home from work. Let's say it was this. Let's say it was mundanity.

You were hanging out your washing, hoping the clouds would give you a stay of execution, when you noticed the swarm of birds whipping panicked shapes into the sky. These were the starlings, murmurating, and you had never seen such a magnificent display.

You moved to the end of your garden for a better look. This was your innocent mistake. That simple movement, that snag from mundanity to something briefly profound, singled you out. The starlings painted a single frame of your watching face in the air, too quick for you to see, then cascaded down and swallowed you.

Remember it? The sudden strike of a million wings on your skin, the skittering shriek of their voices deep in your ear, the wrenching of your hair as the boldest ones grabbed what they could to stop you running? You tried to run, tried to bat those things away and stunned a few, remember? There were two or three of them left behind in your garden as the others lifted you away; black blotches against your lawn like sudden molehills, the last you would ever see of the place where you lived, and ate, and slept, and cried, and loved, and smiled. Just like that.

\*

The starlings took turns holding you, not that you noticed. To keep the momentum of the murmuration going, they had to synchronise with each other, to think as small parts of one whole unit. So, whenever

31

a change of direction was needed, which was often, some would let go and others would dart into place to keep you held. All you knew of this were the tingling pinpricks of claws piercing flesh which, at the time, you put down to a ferocious anxiety of your nerves.

You were fortunate, though. Yours is a coastal town, so the starling journey didn't take long. They carried you over the town centre, and the nature reserve, then executed a gut-flipping plummet over the cliffs, down to the beach. Here they landed, the whole mass of them at once, and you too, face first, the sand banking up into your mouth. The starlings let go and you spent a moment vomiting the beach back onto itself whilst trying to rearrange your brain back into its rightful order.

On the cliff edges, seven magpies cackled at the scene. Five flew closer, attracted by the silver on your wrist and embedded in your ears. They strutted up, planned their approach and then darted in and pecked at the metals until they came away. You didn't have the energy to fight back. I think, in the end, you helped them. Three of the five flew away with your trinkets winking in their beaks. Two remained. They wanted you to feel joyous. Did you? I think, at that moment, you were a twist-ed wreck on a polluted beach and it was hard for you to think much of anything at all. You just wanted to go home, correct? But where exactly is home for a human? We have never been quite sure.

The magpies took to their wings and flashed away. Perhaps you thought that was it: it had all been some elaborate avian thievery to take away your shiny things. Sure, it's a bonus for the magpies, but its more than that. It's better for all of us if you don't have things that remind you of home. You're less likely to try and run away.

The gulls descended from the thermals. They were not so gentle.

*

The passage over the ocean was rough. The gulls, not as keen on working together, kept cawing at each other and dropping you from their beaks. You smashed into the waters more times than you can remember (it was twenty-three), and each fall felt like being hit with an igloo. It shattered you, the smack of brine, the plunge into the murk, and then the frantic ripping of clothes and skin as the gulls hoisted you back up again, sodden, dripping, an ice block just melted.

They had to learn patience that day, the gulls, which is a remark-able achievement for them. So, that's something at least.

*

They took you to this place, to The Island. They circled it a few times, to allow you to see it, get the aspect of it. You witnessed the high mounds of guano at the edges which ring my mountain, and the thick jungle along the slopes. A hazy circle of cloud obscured the peak, and an orchestra of shrieks, chatters, caws, and keens rose from every which place and all wheres.

I got my first glimpse of you. Just a distant shape drooping from tired beaks, but the sight stirred me. My peacocks helped me from my nest and I waddled to the edge of the plateau. The gulls are not worthy to approach, so it would be some time before we were brought together. But you were here now, and I could start to call you mine.

I watched as the gulls chose a place to alight. Right at the furthest point of the Western edge. It stank. You're used to it now, but remem-ber the first time you smelt it? Remember how it pierced the top of your throat, how it reached down and gripped your lungs, how it seemed to burn the walls of your nostrils? Remember retching so hard your rib broke?

The boobies and gannets did not understand. They hobbled in as the gulls took their leave and prodded at your prostate body. They nib-bled at your scalp and slapped at you with the webs of their feet. It took hundreds of them to get you to smarten up, waken up and move out. You were coddled inland and, as you reached the treeline, an albatross barrelled into your back and sent you flying into the jungle. You turned on it, remember? Ready to fight back. Ready to take on the afterlife and every demon it would fling at you.

You had no energy, though. And this isn't the afterlife. But you were so close, at that point, to death. We're sorry about that. We were as gentle as we could possibly be.

I'm sorry it was you. If it hadn't been you, it would've been someone else. Happens all the time. You had a family didn't you? Kids? A partner? Parents, yes? And best friends, lovers, colleagues? Didn't we know that? Of course we did. But you have to understand something

River; we need you more than you need us. So, we have to have this arrangement you see. It's for the best.

*

The parrots took you next. Gentle wings mended you. They brought food, kept you company, tried a few words of your language. Toucans brought you fresh water held in their beaks, which you managed to sip a little of, each time it came. As your senses returned you contemplated a dash back across the guano to the final forgiveness of the sea, but the albatross stalked the edge of the jungle and you didn't dare try.

Birds of Paradise coaxed you deeper into the jungle. They flitted past like living fireworks and your frazzled brain followed the colours until you were hopelessly lost among the vines. You thought you saw snakes, spiders, poisonous frogs, but there was none of this. There were only birds. Strange to think of it that way, isn't it?

The jewels of the jungle kept you salivated and they led you along a weaving path to the mountainside. Far above, I waited; an exemplar of patience. You lay upon the slope and begged for rest. A kettle of vultures swept down. They placed delicate wings over your eyes and granted you the deepest sleep you ever experienced. You were weightless.

*

The vultures gave you to the eagles. The eagles passed you to the condor. The condor took you to the mountain.

To my mountain. As you slept, I waddled out to try and get a proper look. You were still at a distance, so it was hard to see your detail, but even then, I was most pleased. I'd not known excitement like that for years.

I think your eyes fluttered once or twice, and in that half-sleep you might have seen me too. A dark speck on the edge of a cave, flanked by peacocks, guarded by an ostrich. Perhaps a small part of you understood then. That I was yours and you were mine, and we would complete each other. I thought, in that moment, of a name for you. I know how you humans like your words. I chose River because you had flowed

34

to me.

But your journey was not yet over. Each bird must have its turn. I clacked my ancient beak in approval and ostrich passed the signal to condor with a bob of her head. Down you both soared to the steppe of snow, where the sudden cold snapped you back to attention. Condor stayed a while, his wings spread, protecting you from the worst of it. He left as the penguins arrived.

\*

They huddled you in, the emperors, and you all walked together as one. Perhaps you pushed yourself up, clear of the ice, and lay upright, squashed in the down of the penguins. They chattered and cawed at you, our wise old emperors, to help you understand. They told you about me and the death of my mate. About our one remaining egg, about the failures of all the others. I needed companionship, River, I needed friendship. I needed something that the other birds just couldn't quite provide.

I needed that human touch, that intelligence of care. I needed stories and poems, pictures and song. And I needed your violence, River. The crook of your finger, your steady eye, the lust of your blood.

The penguin march was slow and long, they were not so used to waddling in such a close mass. They stopped as night fell and pressed in closer, but their squabbles and skirmishes kept you from falling asleep. A few more hours of trekking after dawn and then you arrived. The emperors pushed and squeezed you out to meet my ostrich at the foot of the final ascent. Reluctant but loyal, the ostrich ushered you onto her back and carried you up to my plateau.

\*

And now here you are.

You are a marvel. The smoothness of your skin, the finery of your golden hair. All the birds of The Island will want to see you and peck beaks at your strange little toes, the funny whorls of your ears, your extra bits of flesh. The peacocks stripped you down to see if you are a male one or female one, but we were not sure. It does not matter.

I am not the most impressive bird. Not the largest, or the most colourful, or the strongest. I cannot fly and I do not have much hope for my last egg. Nor am I smart to the changes of our world. Do you feel it? It is hot when it should be cold, cold when it should be hot. You see why I cannot hope? Perhaps hope is something you can help with, perhaps I am doing it wrong.

I am the last of my kind, unless this egg proves otherwise. This is why I have taken you. I'm sorry it had to be you, but we will take good care of you, I promise. The Island is bountiful with insects and small mammals, you will not go hungry. And loosened feathers will cover blue skin. Wounds will heal. Memories will fade.

And you will not grow bored. Here, on the eastern edge of the plateau we have mounted the rifle. A trophy the clever corvids salvaged from a failed hunting party. Finches clear away the rust and snow. The hummingbirds keep the barrel clean, crows supply bullets for the stock-pile. I trust you know how it works?

Lie here. Your finger on the trigger, that's it. The stock in your shoulder and your eye to the scope. Take a moment to scan the scenery. The jungle, the guano, the plains, the coastline, yes? You will lie here watching and if the dodo hunters come, the parrots will squawl and the hawks will hover above each target.

We will allow you to rest for a few hours each night. You will join me in my nest and we will huddle together over the egg. We can grieve together and hope together. I know I will love you and I think you will love me too. Life is better here, yes? Life makes more sense here.

Imagine if this wasn't you. Imagine if this was someone else. You would be so envious, wouldn't you? To have been one of the unlucky ones, left behind.

But it isn't. It's you. You are mine and I am yours, we are a flock of two. And together, we will hope for the best.

# Come and See the Whale

"Ladies and gentlemen, boys and girls, androgenes and humanes …gather in, gather in…distinguished guests, presslords, Your Majesty. Welcome one and all to London, and to Oceania. It is my great honour to be standing before you all this evening for the grand launch of our latest exhibition. I cannot express to you how excited we are about this momentous occasion. Thank you, thank you.

"Tonight, behind this curtain, you will witness the astonishing accomplishment of a vast team of talented and dedicated individuals far too numerous to list by name…but we love each and every one of you of course! They include the finest minds in the fields of marine science, oceanography, conservation, bioengineering, museum curation…Jane and Teisha down at the front there…erm, neurology, tank construction, metallurgy, animal welfare, cetology and, of course, curtain design… look at the size of that thing!

"But the real star of the show is not the people. It's not the scientists and engineers…or your handsome presenter. It's not even the people who have worked around the clock to make this happen. The real star of this show is Moby. Not, of course, the bald light-listening musician, rest his soul. A different Moby. Someone altogether larger and very much still with us.

"Ladies and gentlemen, boys and girls. People of the glorious human race. It is my overwhelming honour to say these words. Step right up and…come and see the whale!

"No flash photography please, no flashes. Thank you. Feel free to tweet, our hashtag is #MobyWhale.

"Say hello to Moby. Moby is an adult male Physester macrocephalus. A sperm whale in the very prime of his life. We think he's around 45 years old, born in the early 2000s. He is considerably larger than the average male sperm whale at 63ft but, as you can see, fits comfortably in our very special tank…more on the tank in a moment. I'll let you take all this in first.

"Rest assured ladies and gentlemen, this is absolutely a real-life whale. This is not an optical trick; this is not animatronics or CGI. This is a genuine, living, blubber-and-bone sperm whale caught in the Atlantic, about 800 miles due east from Nantucket. You can see there the flukes of the tail pushing through the waters, and at the other end; he's opening his lower jaw...saying hello, look! We're hoping that soon he will show signs of needing to surface and we might be lucky enough to see the blowhole in action. He's real, my friends, he's a real whale.

"And ok, I can hear some murmurs at the back there, some questions. Yes, I'm sure you all have questions, but please allow me to explain. All is not quite what it seems.

"Moby is here with us now, suspended in the carefully-treated waters of our reinforced tank. The glass is a palladium-graphene compound latticed throughout with a filigree titanium mesh, too fine to see with the naked eye, but ultra-strong. We think perhaps it is the strongest glass ever produced; a nuclear warhead wouldn't shatter it. And the water inside the tank is mineralised and heavy-laden to mimic the depths, pressure, temperature and temperament of the Atlantic Ocean. Moby is suspended within these waters, which are replenished daily and continually monitored, but he is very much held in place.

"Please madam yes, yes, let me explain. You see Moby is here, physically, with us in this tank, in this room, in Oceania, in London. But mentally, he is not here. Mentally, he is in his own home, 800 miles off the coast of Nantucket. Simeon, you can put the footage on the screens now, please.

"We will grant access to the walkways in due course but for now, ladies and gentlemen, please refer to the screens above your heads, or log in to the app on your tablets for the live-feed. Here we go. So, this image shows Moby's head from above through the open top of the tank. The great grey mass here is Moby; this circle here is his blowhole. But as you can see...if we zoom in a little...here we go. You can see here...and here...these lines that lead from his head and out of shot, out of the tank. Here we are, five of them...a sixth there.

"And if we lift up...thank you Simeon...and away from the tank, following the cables, up and up, what do we find on the end...? Our puppeteers. Give us a wave guys! Now this here is the real genius of the operation. This is what allows us to take one of the largest creatures on Earth from the depths of his home and place him in a tank for your viewing pleasure. These fine specimens on the computers are our core team of VR developers and programmers. They have, through some sort of magical computer wizardry that I certainly don't claim to understand, encoded a whole and very real world for Moby. These wires, grafted harmlessly into key sensory areas of his brain, feed Moby with his very own Atlantic Ocean.

"Simeon, please show us what Moby can see... there we are. Home. A vast, endless aquatic world, every bit as real to Moby as his life before he came here. To Moby there is no here, there is only there. Our developers have designed a world of such incredible detail that it is virtually indistinguishable from real life itself, especially for a whale who knows no different. Our core cluster of nodes attach to the thalamus of Moby's brain and feed sensory data to the optic nerve, the olfactory system and the pyramidal tract to process Moby's version of reality to his eyes, his nasal passage, and his spinal cord and so on. To mimic the sperm whale's particular talent for echolocation we've rigged a highly advanced sonar system into the eastern end of the tank in the direction Moby faces. This is SELIT, or the Spatial EchoLocate Interwave Terminus. Moby sends his calls to SELIT and SELIT sends the echo back, based on what is ahead of him in the virtual Atlantic. And, if that is another whale, well then SELIT sends a call right on back. We'll do you a demonstration at the end of the tour and you'll be able to hear and feel it for yourselves, all being well.

"To all intents and purposes Moby entirely believes he is swimming through the Atlantic Ocean. At regular intervals throughout the day Moby is 'successful' in hunting plankton from the seabed and we wash real plankton through our filters to keep him fed – and that is an awful lot of plankton, but we've got it under control. Of course, the sperm whale is the largest predator in the world so Moby can't survive on plankton alone. We serve up regular dishes of squid and ray, but only when he's been successful hunting them in his world. Again, we have a demonstration lined up later.

"It is our belief, and we hope you'll share this, that Moby is actually better off here with us than he would be out in the wild. Here there is never any danger of him being hunted by man for his bones or his oils. Nor will he feel the effects of a poisoned sea as we continue to choke our oceans with plastic waste and chemicals. And not only is this great for Moby, it's an incredible opportunity for our scientists. Here at Oceania, with your kindly donations and sponsorships, the leading cetologists can get up close and personal with a sperm whale like never before. There are still so many mysteries surrounding the sperm whale and his brethren, simply because they are so damn hard to get close to for any length of time. Here with us, scientists, thinkers, artists - they have all the time in the world to be with Moby. As do you. Here at Oceania we are dedicated to our free entry – we only ask for donations and monthly direct debits if you can afford them. Anything you can spare will go directly to Moby, directly to this magnificent, world-leading and living exhibition of scientific research.

"And, we can say with the fullness of confidence that Moby, himself, is happy. Never before in the history of captivity could we ever truly say that the animal in the cage, or the tank, or the enclosure was completely happy. Not completely. Now we can say that. Moby has his life and we have Moby. This moment, my companions, could be one of the most significant advances in the history of animal science; in the history of science full stop.

"And! Well, I'm not supposed to tell you this but... ok, Jane is nodding. Moby is but the first. In our New York branch work has started already on a tank twice this size and our next prize is a fully-grown adult blue whale, the largest creature on Earth. We've already got a few candidates identified. And from there, who knows? A great white shark? A giant squid? The possibilities are endless. We have the technology but, more importantly, we have the passion. We have the vision.

"Moby swims into his future and leads us with him. No more is this magnificent beast enslaved to the whims and ways of frivolous human beings. He is the essence of freedom, an emblem of a brighter tomorrow for both his kind, and mankind. The possibilities of this technology are endless. We see visions of great ocean mammals rescued from the brink of extinction. We see a worldwide revival of appreciation and respect for the beautiful creatures who share our planet. We see animals no longer in captivity but liberated into better worlds. We see a better world for all. And we hope you see it too. Ladies, gentlemen, thank-"

And then. There was a power cut.

# Betamorphosis

*In 2013, neuroscientists Tim Marzullo and Greg Gage launched a Kickstarter campaign to fund 'RoboRoach': a method of attaching electrodes to the brain of a live cockroach, which could then be controlled by a phone app.*

When Gxyrx Gxyrxsyn awoke one morning from troubled dreams, he found himself changed into a 1997 Lara Croft. He was standing upright, his forelegs pointed straight out in front, on the ends of which he could see crude hands clutching cruder pistols. He could just about see the jagged points of a pair of polygon breasts on the front of his thorax. Most curiously of all, he could not smell anything, nor could he feel any vibrations through his legs, which now numbered four rather than six. He tried to move, but couldn't even turn his head.

He was in the largest hangar room, where lights shifted and colours shimmered, but at present it was blank. Snaking along the ground he could see a thick black line which trailed to a pair of silhouetted figures in the distance. Of course, in a normal state of affairs, he would have fled at the sight of the humans, but as he could not move there was nothing he could do but stand and stare.

He knew, at least, that he was not far from the nest. Gxyrx was a waterscout and he had recently discovered a plentiful supply in a distant cavity three rooms over. He had been most pleased with his find. The latest hatching of nymphs had swelled their numbers considerably and the swarm needed a new home. Gxyrx's discovery had great potential, and he'd been excitedly laying a trail of faeces to help the other scouts when some strange obstruction had fallen in his way: a circle of glass walls. He had been trying to climb it, before a strange force lifted his body and carried him away. A sudden exhaustion had seized him, and he'd tumbled into the troubled dreams before waking to this. He desperately hoped his clan would come looking for him and find the trail. His father and mother, Ax and Ox, should not be too far away, and his beloved sister, Gonymph, would be close behind.

And then he moved. He swivelled to his left. But he had not told himself to move: someone else had done it for him. He moved again:

forward, back, a jolt to the right. The sensation was most peculiar; like he was being blown by a wind without feeling it.

"Whatever has become of me?" he thought, just as one of the pistols flashed and banged. His arms lowered, then raised again, then lowered again. He turned, stepped sideways, then was launched into the air in a strangely weightless leap. When he landed, his mouth opened and closed, but he did not speak. The humans and the black line were now out of his sight, but he presumed it was they who controlled his movements. He did not understand how or why.

He was pushed into a long sprint to the far wall, then swung left just as he reached it. The controllers swept him along the edge of the room, then dragged him in a wide circle to the centre. He was forced to jump for no apparent reason, whipped back, whirled around, ducked, dodged, pushed and yanked, and for a particularly tiresome period, his head was shoved down and he spun and spun and spun until he was quite dizzy. On it went, back and forth, up and down, from the tiles of the floor to the burning glare of the lights; walls that seemed to lurch at him then shrink away, a ceiling that looked to be crashing down one moment, then as distant as the sky the next. The black line lashed, his hind legs screamed with pain, his eyes seemed to melt into the blur, and then, quite suddenly, he was stopped. There, a short scuttle away, was the crack that led to the nest. And there were his family, peering out. His father Ax, his mother Ox and, behind them, her feelers flat to her head, his sister Gonymph. What did they see? Did they understand it was him? Could they do anything to help?

All he really needed them to do was cross the space and taste his trail. He would be content as long as the cavity was discovered; that was the most important thing. He was sure he would soon be released and he would stop being Lara Croft and he would return to his clan, to the swarm, and everything would be correct and proper and right again. But Ax and Ox and Gonymph made no indication that they recognised him and before too long he was swept away once again.

He was sprinted to the centre of the room and stopped. One of the humans moved away from the other and leaned into a glowing device set upon a table. In a silent instant, the room was transformed around him. Where there had once been bright white space, there were now grey and brown blocks, shaded to look textured, with swathes of green on top. The floor took on a muddy hue, and some parts became blue. Water? The thought thrilled him for a fleeting moment, but he knew it was nothing of the sort. He'd spent days scuttling through this room in his normal body; these blocks and patches of blue were nothing more than clever tricks of light. The real floor lay beneath and it too was changed; small, raised areas, tiny towers, pits and depressions. The humans were able to change the shape of the floor however they so wished, but only into small structures. The reasons for why had never bothered Gxyrx until now.

Slowly, he was walked to the nearest block, which was only slightly taller than him in his Lara Croft form. He was jumped and his arms flung up and connected with the edge of the block. He hung there for a moment and then felt a sharp ache in his foreleg joints as they folded and pushed him to the top. His hindlegs followed and he was soon standing on top of the block, looking out over the rest of the transformed hangar. But he was given no time to take in the view. A great leap brought him crashing to the ground again, and then he was running. He was flung at another block and felt the same sting in his joints as the controllers pulled him up. This block connected to the next one via a walkway, which he was promptly sprinted across.

At the next block, his forelegs were lifted. Pivoting wildly from the middle of his thorax, he saw the guns had reappeared and were pointing each and every way, before he was stopped and his forelegs — which he now realised he should think of as arms, human arms — were dropped to his sides again.

There followed another period of inertia. Drained, he wanted nothing more than to scuttle back into his nest and bury his head beneath the abdomen of a slumbering roach before being woken for the migration to the new cavity. From up here he could see distant, dark specks of other cockroaches but his running and climbing had been so disorientating, and the room had been changed so much, he could not tell if those specks were anywhere near his trail, nor where his trail actually was. He hoped he was not to be the Lara Croft for so much longer.

Then he saw something else move. Something much bigger. It was a jagged, grey shape which trotted into the centre of the hangar and raised its head to look around. It appeared to be a dog of some sort, cut from the same design as the environment. He thought it must be another projection of light, however it was one that could move around and perform actions, much like he could, in a sense. He wondered if another pair of humans was now controlling this dog and if it too had once been a real creature, a real dog.

It paced around for a while then drew a little closer to the block where Gxyrx stood watching. Then Gxyrx's arms were raised, pointed at the dog, and the pistols flashed and banged. The dog made a small attempt to run but was quickly felled. It lay dead for a short while before it disappeared. A moment later, so did everything else.

\*

The hangar was silenced, darkened and reduced to its normal blank state. Gxyrx felt a thrill of excitement shoot through his brain stem. This was it; he was to be freed and could continue on with his work for the swarm. He heard the footsteps of the humans as they left the hangar, but as the door clicked shut behind them, Gxyrx was still unable to move. His sight was still much higher in the air than normal, which meant he remained in the Lara Croft form. Why had he been left this way?

He heard a voice.

"Gxyrx! What's happening, Gxyrx?"

It was his beloved sister, Gonymph! She was not yet at her second moult and yet she was clever and kind. Gxyrx tried to call out to her;

"Gonymph, I am here! It is me!" But nothing sounded, nothing in his mouth moved at all.

"Gxyrx, our mother and father are so worried. You have not come back from your expedition, and yet you are due to go on another very soon! You've been allocated to join the Eastern Wall Quorum, but they leave in a few hours, Gxyrx. You must go with them; it is such a good opportunity for you. Our father says it is so!"

And so his trail had not been discovered. Otherwise, there would be no Eastern Wall expedition; all efforts would be focused on his cavity discovery to the South and the subsequent plans for migration. If only he could tell Gonymph! Perhaps if she followed the black line — which Gxyrx could still see at the edge of his sight — she would find the controller and find some way of using it so he could, at the very least, be guided to the nest. Someone among the clans might find a way to communicate with him or stop him being Lara Croft for a while.

"I can smell that you are close by, Gxyrx, please come out..."

She appeared in his sight. There was no mistaking her pale abdomen, her delicate antennae. She would grow to become such a beautiful cockroach. She looked up at him, tasting the air with her palpi, but she did not recognise that the Lara Croft was actually he, her brother Gxyrx, silently screaming for movement.

"Oh, Gxyrx," she said, as she scurried back towards the nest, "I hope you are well. But I must fetch our parents. I simply must."

He waited for what felt like many hours, but must only have been mere minutes. His sense of time was difficult to keep track of when he had spent so long not being able to move. Gonymph appeared again in the same place. This time she had Ax and Ox with her. Ax stepped forward.

"Gxyrx. Son. This is your father. Time to stop this nonsense now."

"Come on out dear," said Ox, but Ax raised his antenna to silence her.

"Son, this is no time for illness or shyness. You are to represent our clan, Gxyrx. It is a great honour. A Quorum, son! You know how important this is."

Gxyrx's brain stem felt fit to burst. He was pushing so hard to break from his Lara Croft body. Of course he wanted to join the Quorum! Of course it was a great honour! He had so much to give to the swarm right now! But there was nothing he could do. No matter how hard he willed it, he could not shift even half an inch.

"Please, Gxyrx," said Ox. His mother's voice as fragile as a nymph's first hind wing. "You can hear how much this means to your father! This is no time to be selfish."

His will drained and his mind went limp. It was no use. He was stuck in this form, perhaps forever. Presently, his father clicked his disapproval and scuttled away. Ox followed. Gonymph lingered for a while longer. She seemed to be staring up at the Lara Croft, this curious new shape she had not seen before this day. Eventually, she turned away too, clicking her sadness as she meandered back to the nest.

*

The night was agonisingly slow, but it passed. He was not visited
again, although he heard the thunder of feet as the Eastern Wall Quorum
departed for the expedition.

He could feel himself growing quite ill. It was the worst thing for
a cockroach, to be on his or her own for too long a time. The senses dull,
the legs weaken, the mind slips. Many a cockroach has died when stuck
alone, lost or captured. Gxyrx was beginning to believe he was most
likely in the latter category.

The hangar room was lightened again in a series of brief flickers.
The door opened and closed and he heard the humans enter. Gxyrx wondered what performances would be expected of him today. He hoped
they would guide him closer to the controller so he could take a good
look at it. Perhaps he could find a way to shoot it, or shoot the humans.
There must be something he could do.

It did not take long for the movement to start again, and he was
surprised to find himself immensely glad of it. At least now something
was happening; at least time could flow properly once more. He was
run around the space for a while, to the far wall and back, and in wide
circles again. He jumped a few times, shot a few bullets to the air with
no lasting effect on the ceiling or anything else. Twice he swung near to
the humans, saw their faces, smiling, and caught brief glimpses of the
controller, but he came no closer to any sort of understanding.

After a short while, the transformation of the room took place.
This time it was the four walls that changed the most. They became a
mottled grey, while the floor took on the colour of coffee dust. Two
large striped columns rose from the floor to the ceiling, both of which
were far too high to leap on. He was turned and hurried up a rise of
steps to a mezzanine that overlooked a small floor space. Yesterday, the
transformed hangar had felt somewhat like the outdoors – colours like
grasses and patches of mud – but now he felt he was inside; a room with
a ceiling and doorways.

Two dogs appeared and his fore- no, his arms, raised to shoot
them. The dogs were much faster than the one yesterday and his first few
shots missed their mark. One of the dogs ran up the steps towards him,
so he was pushed off the mezzanine to escape, falling into the path of the

other dog. A few more shots fired – one struck, the others missed – and the dog leapt up to him, its strange mouth open, teeth bared. He was backed away, guns blaring, until most of the invisible bullets struck their mark and the leaping dog was stopped.

He was turned to see the other dog running fast down the steps but one further quick flash-bang of the pistol slammed it to the wall with a yelp. An 'x' shape replaced its eye and it slid down the stairs as if they were smooth. Gxryx heard one of the humans cheer and clap.

Gxryx could feel pain piercing through him as if he had been shot, or bitten somehow by the polygon dog. He was walked forward and his head was titled down to look closer at the corpse of the dog. The sudden swing of sight made him dizzy again. He wanted nothing more than to close his eyes and stop the movement, shut away the sight of the dead dog, all of it and everything. But he could not. And then, just at the bottom edge of his sight, he saw something most curious. He saw a cockroach.

It was not Ax or Ox, nor was it Gonymph, but he could tell from the curve of the wings, the shade of brown, the stubbiness of the cerci at the rear, that it was a roach of his clan – perhaps an uncle or cousin – and yet, there was something most peculiar about the head. There did not appear to be one. Or, at least, it was obscured by this other construction – a flat silver panel of sorts, with green lines and miniscule wires instead of antennae.

As his head was swung back up the realisation fell down to meet him. It was he, himself. It was Gxryx. The metal panel was the thing that had his body controlled. It was the thing that made him Lara Croft.

The room changed. The columns twisted away and became open space and the walls faded. The floor collapsed, but gently, to create a deep pit which was quickly filled by an azure blue. The mezzanine remained for a moment longer, then blinked out. Gxryx was pushed forward into another run, and then he was forced into the blue pit. As he descended his view was pushed down and he saw himself plummeting, unable to flick out his wings. The blue light closed around him, and all his movements thickened. There appeared to be no surface to land on. He was pushed forward and his Lara-arms waved at the blueness and pushed it behind. It was supposed to be water, Gxryx noted, although not with any great surprise or excitement. He had become dulled by the whole experience, absorbed by exhaustion and sickness.

Deeper and deeper he descended,  the world becoming the wholeness of this blue and nothing more, save for the sweeping of his Lara-arms and her misshapen hands. He dreamed of real water, of the leaky pipe near the nest, of the sinks in the washrooms and the dampness in the kitchen walls.

Gxryx came to a stop as he appeared to strike against the base of the pit, although he did not feel it. His Lara-arms began to flail, although he did not feel this either. The Lara body began to make strange choking noises and he realised she was drowning. Would they not take him and her back to the surface? Was this to be the end of the experiment? He felt nothing as Lara died. Her weightless figure collapsed around his mind.

*

Gxryx awoke to the sound of his sister's voice.

"Gxryx, are you there? Oh brother, please say you are!"

The room was white and blank once again, the blue pit and dog corpses gone, as if never there at all. Gxryx stayed consciously still for a moment, then tried to move. He could not. At the edge of his sight he could see the peaks of his Lara Croft breasts. It was not possible for him to die yet.

"Gxryx, the Quorum expedition was a great success! They found a rich food source which will feed us all for a long, long time. I've brought some along. Perhaps you are hungry?"

Gxryx was hungrier than he had ever known and wished dearly for a morsel of the food. He tried to picture the movements of Lara Croft in his mind, perhaps to trick the panel upon his head into making her and himself step forward. But the inertia persisted.

"Perhaps if I leave it for you. Here, beside this statue. I shall leave it and you can come out in your own time to eat it? Would you like that Gxryx?"

Beside a statue? Could she mean Lara? And then, for a very brief moment, he caught the scent of something... of rotted fruit. Apple, or pear perhaps. She was so close! Just a few steps more!

"Gxryx? Is that... is that you, brother?"

Yes! It is me! He strained to nuzzle her, to flick his antennae against hers. She shrieked and the sound seemed to tear Gxryx into two clean pieces.

"Oh Gxryx! What has become...? I am sorry, I cannot look!"

She clicked her mandible but stayed close. A moment later, he heard a soft scrape close to his head. A sensation pressed against his palpi and filled his mouth. It felt strange, like it had come through the tips of his claws — the toes of Lara's feet — and travelled through his legs and his thorax to reach his mouth. It was taste. It was apple. Gonymph had pushed the apple to his face and he must have opened his mouth, quite without thinking. He concentrated on the movement, which he could not feel, but he could imagine with precise accuracy. The sounds confirmed that he was indeed eating the flesh of the apple. He imagined himself saying 'thank you', but no words were spoken. She would know. Gonymph his clever, clever sister.

"I will go now," she said, between clicks. "I will bring father and mother again, and perhaps they will know what to do. I am so very sorry Gxryx."

After a short while, Gxryx realised she was gone. He had not heard her leave through the sounds of mashing apple.

Only his father visited. Not his mother, and if Gonymph had followed, she did not make a sound. For too long a while, his father was silent. Finally, he spoke.

"Gxryx, this is most inappropriate."

The apple taste faded. Either it was all eaten or the apple had been pulled away by his father. Gxryx suspected the latter. He hoped Gonymph had saved more food for him. His father opened and snapped his wings shut, as was his manner when distressed.

"Most inappropriate, son. Let it be known, I had great hopes for you. I did not want this for you, but look what has become. You have greatly disappointed your mother."

Snap-snap went the wings. Tap, tap, the impatient fall of his father's feet as he paced.

"And you gave your sister such a fright! She is quite unwell now, and all the nymphs turn their wings from her in shame. A shunned daughter! And...this is from our son!"

51

Gxryx realised his mouth might still be open, his palpi prodding for apple. He imagined the movements of his palpi retracting and his mouth closing and hoped against hope that it had happened.

"You have made it quite sure, son, that we shall never hear of Quorum recruitment again."

For a long while, all went quiet and Gxryx assumed that he was alone. But then the snapping resumed, more furious than before, and a few final words came to his head from Ax, his father.

"There is chatter of a second discovery, greater than the first. A cavity to the south, large enough for the whole swarm. We migrate tomorrow. I do not expect you to join us."

*

When the humans returned, Gxryx was surprised to discover that he hadn't died in the night. He'd long thought himself passed into death; just an endless blank whiteness with no sound, no taste, no movement, nothing. As the room transformed into stone, sand, grass tufts, and still pools, Gxryx felt as if he was being born into a new life, and now he really was Lara Croft, as if he had never been a cockroach and his previous life had all been some great fantasy, a mindless dream.

He ran, he climbed, he swam in shallow pools, he shot into the air, and into the dogs, and other creatures. For a long while he was faced with a large wall, sections of which could be rotated and pushed around. He allowed himself to imagine the feeling of touching, turning, pulling the tiles of the wall and his mind, at least, began to feel it physically. The roughness, the weight, the resistance of the scrape. After many incorrect combinations, the patterns on the tiles formed a symmetrical symbol of sorts and, away to his left, something large and heavy creaked open. He was turned to the sound; a doorway leading into the depths of a sand-coloured building had revealed itself. He wanted very much to go through the door and, after believing that he could, it happened.

Inside, more running, climbing, shooting and, for the first time, he was swung from one level to another via a dangling vine. He rather enjoyed the sensation, but the action was not soon repeated. Twice he and Lara fell from too great a height and they were taken into blackness together, before snapping back to life once more at the same starting place. With each restart, he felt himself becoming the woman more and more; so much so, that he longed for her death again just to allow him a few more mental steps towards becoming her completely. He envied the thrill of her life, the discoveries that lay before her.

They were bested by a pack of the dogs and she died again. Gxryx was almost there, he was almost Lara, when there came an interruption and it was all shattered. He heard the familiar scuttle of cockroach feet, and a tiny voice that seemed to lodge itself inside him like a bullet in a dog.

"Gxryx," said Gonymph. "Oh brother! Is there nothing you can do?"

And so it was true. He had been a cockroach, and he still was. He wanted to say; "Have you brought me any food? If not, then you should leave." He did not want his sister any longer. He wanted Lara.

"Gxryx, the swarm leaves soon. Did father tell you? We've found a new cavity."

He was moved away from Gonymph but she followed and stayed as close to him as she could bear. He remembered the cavity; the moistness of the air, the soggy sections of wall, the peeling paint. Warmth and safety. The place he had discovered, him alone. It seemed so long ago and far away. Worlds away from this playground, his desert of light.

"Father said you could still come. If you stopped this sickness and apologised to the clan, they might still let you. Can I tell them, Gxryx? Can I tell them you apologise?"

He was stopped at a closed gate. Beside the gate were five switches fixed into the ground. He and Lara were supposed to throw the switches in a particular order to open the gate. Gxryx did not know the sequence, and he suspected Lara did not either. He was walked to switch three, then five, then four, two, one. It did not work. All the while, Gonymph stayed with him.

"Please, brother," she whispered, "please!"

Every combination that was tried did not open the gate. It became tiresome to keep throwing switches. Who was keeping track of the sequences they had already tried? Who was not clever enough to work this out?

He was stopped and the world faded back. The lights fuzzed

and flickered. The switches became cross-hatched models of themselves and were swapped around. The gate blinked on and off, slid open and slammed shut. But he, Gxryx, was held at some strange distance from it all, as if set aside and frozen. Gonymph continued to plead with him, her voice more and more fragile.

A thought came to Gxryx. He wanted now to be Lara, but he did not want to be controlled. And yet he missed his old life too. He did want to apologise to the clan, to the whole swarm. Perhaps he could not go with them, but if only they were to understand his difficulty, they would forgive him. And that forgiveness may extend to Ax and Ox, and to Gonymph of course.

He used the feelers of his mind to reach out and explore the insides of the Lara body. He touched the jagged contours of her inner shoulders, and the bends of her knees. He imagined, then felt, the weight of the pistols in her hands. In his hands. He scratched and scraped and pressed each bend and fold of her until the picture was complete inside his head. And then he pushed her forward, as if she was just in front of him and, together, they moved. And it was he, Gxryx that made them move, not the black line, not the humans.

He turned away from the switches and looked down at Gonymph. Her wings had darkened, her latest moult nearly off. Soon she would be an adult roach, her name would become Goryx, her role would be assigned. Her compound eyes glistened with hope and fear. He tried to say 'Come, sister' but the voice did not work, Lara's mouth did not move.

He ran. He passed through the blocks of light, he flew over a pit of blue light, he ignored the advance of an angry hound. He saw the gap for the nest to his right and bolted for it.

And there, on the threshold, his father and mother waited. Ox's antennae twitched and whirled, Ax stepped forward, mouth parts clacking. Gxryx gave a giddy skip as he drew closer and brought Lara down to her knees to crawl up to the loving nuzzle of his forgiving parents - but then he saw the look upon his father's face. Ax rose up to the tips of his claws and opened his wings as wide as he could manage. Ox retreated into the shadow of the nest.

Gxryx skidded to a stop. Gonymph crashed into him from behind. She too saw the look on their father's face.

"Daughter, come away," bellowed Ax.

"Father, I-"

"Gonymph," came the meek voice of Ox, "come to me now. We'll keep you safe."

"Go to your mother. Come away from this fiend."

Gonymph stepped away from Gxryx and whispered a word to him so faint he did not catch it. She ran clicking to the forbidden space behind their father's wings.

"You will leave."

Gxryx shuffled forward, just an inch. Ax regarded the being before him, every fractured polygon of Gxryx's new and strange body. He leapt to the air, hissed, screeched and flitted his wings.

"You will leave!"

Gxryx turned away. He looked for shade, for any patch of darkness to hide in. But there was none. He stood Lara up and walked her away until he could no longer hear his father hissing.

A figure walked over to meet them. A human. The human moved too fast for Gxryx to see detail but he saw the hairs of its face, the flash of lenses over its eyes. It ducked down, out of sight, and Gxryx tried to flee but immediately crashed into a wall which had not been there before.

His Lara body disappeared. The shapes of the world fuzzed, stretched, then flattened. He saw a symbol of himself waiting on the flat part of the universe. There was only one way to go; to the right, along an endless line, upon which there were blocks of different heights and sizes, steps leading up and down, pitfalls, spikes, and flagpoles. He ran along the line, looking for an end, which never came.

*

Gonymph went searching for her brother one last time before the migration. She only had a few minutes to spare; the swarm was nearly ready.

The lights of the hangar room had been changed into yet another set of strange shapes and she was quickly disorientated. She kept having to loop her way back to the nest and start out again, just so she didn't get lost.

Was there any hope left for Gxryx? He had seemed so keen to come back and make his apology, but father could not stand for it. He had explained to her, and to their mother; that thing is no longer your brother. Your brother is gone. But he could not be gone, he still smelled the same and looked mostly the same.

A light-human ran past her, but it was not Gxryx. This one had smoother edges, browner legs, a flatter chest. Something above Gonymph flashed and the light-human ducked behind a small wall. Gonymph ran the opposite way.

A large black line swung across the ground towards her but she skipped over it easily. She knew Gxryx had a line attached to the... thing on his head, so she turned and followed it. The line snapped and slithered across the ground and it was quite the effort to keep up with its wild movements. A small panic began to settle into Gonymph as she felt herself get further and further away from the nest.

Finally, the line lifted from the ground and disappeared above her, but she could not see her brother anywhere. In fact, it had grown quite dark. She found a flat surface nearby and crawled up it to the top. From here she could see out to where a human was watching a glowing screen. The human was pressing and pushing a device with its hands and the black line was attached to the device. Gonymph tried to understand, but it was beyond her. She suddenly felt so weak, and stupid.

She turned away from the human and looked out across the hangar. There was the thing Gxryx had become; a light-human, in a lady shape. She had a name of some kind, a place within the human world. She was running through the space, hiding behind towers of light and every so often she would lift her hands and they would flash. The other light-human was there too, a male with smoother edges. His hands flashed too. They flashed at each other across the strange shimmering space.

And far beyond that she saw distant dark specks crowded next to the nest. The specks clustered, then a line formed and the migration began. A long thin line to a far and distant end, a new beginning.

Gxryx's light-human collapsed to the ground and blinked out. She reappeared at the far western edge of the hangar. Soon, her hands were flashing again.

Gonymph said a few words for the brother she had once had. Then she leapt from the platform and ran, breathless, to rejoin her clan, to put the whole sorry thing behind her.

And as she reached them, her mother and father, Ox and Ax, raised their antennae to greet her and remarked on how well she looked, and how she had blossomed recently, despite of all the troubles, into a sleek and attractive cockroach with a bright future. They chittered at each other, their brain-stems warmed at the thought of their beautiful child almost ready to produce nymphs of her own. And Gonymph ran on ahead, flexed her young carapace, stretched her wings, and shook off the very last fragments of her final moult.

# Hutched

On the first day they buy the hutch. The latest design; impenetrable Perspex, wood-effect steel, scent reduction valves, waste siphons, feely-holes automatically airlocked into place when stroking and/or feeding is finished. Solar-powered lighting with one corner bathed in shadow for hiding. Metal rim charged by moonlight to deliver a powerful shock to any midnight fox looking for a meal. High cost, but low maintenance. Nothing gets in or out; perfectly secure and a compact size to fit neatly into even the smallest garden. Optional heating add-on for when winter comes.

He forks out the money and two shop assistants carry it to his car - he shifts Easter eggs from the boot so they can fit it in. Only then do they go back inside the shop and buy a rabbit.

*

On the second day she is reaching in to give it a carrot and when her arm comes back out, she starts scratching it. The rabbit, Flopsy, is the cutest one the shop had. Female, probably. Nicely patterned fur, twitchy nose, white bob tail, lop-ears. It looks happy to be safe now; secure and owned, snuggling into sawdust, like it would in the wild.

But she can't stop scratching, the girl, and by her bedtime her skin is red raw and breaking out in blotches. He pumps her full of drugs and keeps her indoors. She spends the night building up a furious resentment to her new pet, vows never to touch it again.

He, her Dad, checks the internet. He can get an add-on, apparently; a hypoallergenic filter that layers the insides of the hutch and protects against the creature's fur whenever touching is required or desired.

He orders it for next-day delivery.

*

On the third day the filter is fixed in place while Flopsy wriggles in his arms. The girl watches from her bedroom window. It's a grey day so she won't come outside.

The delivery men take less than an hour to apply the filter and reseal the hutch. The rabbit seems happier now. It hops from one end to the other, sniffing. He slots a handful of carrots in for it, a big handful, just in case he doesn't get chance to feed it tomorrow, because of the football and that.

*

On the fourth day, it's the football. Flopsy spends the day alone.

*

On the fifth day, the daughter is persuaded back outside. She watches Flopsy for a bit, tapping at the Perspex. Flopsy doesn't really respond. The rabbit spends most of the time at the back of the hutch in the shadow, hunched up and quiet. The daughter quickly gets bored, asks for a puppy instead.

The man says 'No' but thinks: maybe.

The daughter stamps back inside, angry, and the man watches the rabbit for a while longer while he mows the lawn. He slots in another carrot. Flopsy doesn't respond. She must feel overwhelmed by the size of the hutch, he thinks.

He checks the manual. There is a size reduction mechanism. He finds the control panel in the base and types in the required dimensions. The hutch whirrs as it reconstitutes itself.

Two hours later it is half the size it was. Much cosier. Flopsy seems happier now as she shifts herself to another corner and takes a bite from the carrot.

He watches her eat and checks the manual again. He can get an add-on that automatically feeds it that muesli stuff twice every day. He orders it for next-day delivery.

*

On the sixth day, he fits the feeder and fills it with six-month's worth of food. It comes with a free condenser that extracts moisture from the air so the rabbit can have a fresh supply of water every day. He fits that too.

He steps back, admires the construction; the organic whole of it. He reads up about the other add-ons. The heater. The CCTV. The vitamin mist. The hologram companion. The moult reverser. He orders them all, proud of himself for some indistinct reason. His wife would've been impressed.

In the afternoon, he takes his daughter to the puppy farm.

*

On the seventh day, he fits a few of the gadgets while his daughter plays with Tyler, the staffie.

He doesn't notice Flopsy in the corner, the dark corner, the shadow corner, twitching her nose at him, her ears thrust forward at the sound of his banging, at the sounds of the daughter squealing, at the sounds of Tyler barking.

He switches the hologram on and an image of a wild rabbit appears next to Flopsy. It shifts through a loop of running, grooming, and sleeping. To Flopsy it looks like diffractions of seismic light, hazeform and spectral, unscented; intangible and silent. She can't make ear nor bob tail of it, but it is precisely what she has been waiting for.

Tyler spends hours watching her, slobbering. He gets a shock on his nose as the moon comes up.

*

On the fifteenth day, he checks on her and she is gone.

*

61

On the fifteenth day, she awaits the solar charge, a withered foot resting on the compacted chute of the feeder, ready to pull. She has rewired it into a circuit switch, shutting off the food supply. She has re-configured the arm of the condenser also to redirect the water for engine coolant, sacrificed a third of her space in the hack of the resize mechanism to establish a power grip on the space-time grid. Sunlight seems to coat her eyes. She tries to breathe it in for strength. She is weak with hunger, her heart strains to keep her going. She can feel her skeleton quivering, urging her to collapse. She focuses instead on the temperature, counting off each degree as the morning warms up.

Beneath her, diagrams and formulae she has etched into the hypoallergenic filter using her claws and teeth. The results dictate that she must hold on, just a little longer.

The conductors of the hologram hum as they take in the stores of electricity from the outer shell. She raises one back foot and thumps down the compaction of waste in the clogged siphon. It is the ballast she needs for accurate landing.

And she waits; eyes on the bedroom window beyond the Perspex, beyond the garden.

Finally, the inhabitants of the house wake and stretch, and Flopsy can take no more. She flips the switch and the hutch disappears.

*

On the fifteenth day, the daughter wakes to a thumping heart as her wardrobe explodes and her bed collapses. For half a moment, she is suspended in air. Her stomach plummets and her mouth drops to a scream which is never heard because a hutch, all wires and smells and dried piles of faeces, appears and encloses her body and voice into a tight package. It takes them both, rabbit and girl, to somewhere else; somewhere far, far away.

*

On the fifteenth day, he checks and she is gone.

*

On the fifteenth day, she lands face down in grass and the hutch breaks away from her and disappears into the ether, and then to nothingness. She sits up and looks. A wide field, stretching to every horizon, describing the curve of the world, fuzzing into the crest of the sky.

In between her and that distance, rabbits emerge from warrens, curious. Some creep forward and stand on their hind legs for a better look.

She watches them watching her watching them.

Some start the morning's forage, others thump out messages to companions, but their activities are muted while this new presence sits, observing them like some hunter or rival; some kind of threat, some kind of foe.

But she doesn't move. For hours and hours, she sits and watches, and does nothing else. And as the sun reaches its peak, the rabbits return to their warrens to sleep through the heat. Later, as the light wanes and the day cools, they come back out to eat again. Still she waits, until the first of the evening stars appears in the sky and then, only then, does she get up, stretch her legs, and head over to join them.

# A Time Before Horses

Stabled, I watch the creature stalk the inn. It is a stooped thing and six-limbed: two legs, four arms. Hairless but solid, I can see through its flesh to the insides. Its organs glow, bleeding colours, and its frame of bones is shock-white. It is blind. No: it is eyeless. It sniffs its way with a desperate, wriggling flap of a nose. It skirts the edges of the windows and blends its lights with those of the inn. It is hungry.

If it has smelt me, it does not seem to care. It wants the humans. It can taste them on the air. I know that stench, it's hard to miss.

I watch the thing as it lopes around. I want to get closer, see it properly, smell it, but my tether holds me here. It followed us. I first spied it nestled in an oak six gallops back. Master did not see it. No human saw it. Only me.

I know what it is. In the depths of my guts, in the chatter of my teeth and the flick of my tail; the whole of me knows what it is. But I could be wrong. I hope I am wrong. But if I am right, I need help.

The stable is on a strong wayline; future and past are both sharp. I crack my hoof hard onto stone three times and connect. I thump my heart to the pulse, whip my tail against the rhythm and grind my back teeth to anchor the line. The call to Equus is made. I wait.

All is still for nine minutes. It is a nine minutes which do not exist because I am clenching time between my teeth. The creature is frozen, three arms raised to reach the roof of the inn. It looks like a comet, or a drawing of a star.

A horse of times to come appears to my right. He is a Roann, huge and pristine, with sleek muscles and a thick neck. He blows his lips in greeting but his roving eyes avoid looking at me or the creature. Despite his size, he is nervous. I can see his whip-marks and the poise in his hocks. I flush. I am in the presence of a thoroughbred.

Another horse appears on my left. She is a Blacketts from times gone. She is small and delicate and utterly still. Her flesh is worn with scars and she has no strength across her back. She is not tethered. No bits or straps or shoes, nor any sign of them. She is just here, as if she had always been so. Her cold eyes are fixed on the creature.

I release my teeth and Equus lets time flow again. The creature throws up its fourth arm and grips the roof. It hoists itself up.

I greet Roann and Blacketts. Roann tosses his head up and down and strains towards me to nibble at my neck. He can't quite reach around the half-door of his stable and I am held by my tether. I bow to him instead and shake my head. He chatters.

Blacketts taps her forehoof. It is so silent a greeting I almost miss it. She intends for us to be quiet. Roann snorts.

What is it? he is asking.

Blacketts taps again: quiet.

And we are, for a long while. The creature seems to be enjoying itself on the roof. It scuttles to the chimney and embraces the stack with all four arms. Above, meat-smoke muddies the twilight. The creature's nose is hunting the scent and near to finding it. I worry that it might fit down the hole.

The humans roar and squeal inside the inn, oblivious. A cold chill drops in my timezone and I shiver. For Roann it must be warmer because he is sweating. Blacketts does not flinch, not even to rid herself of the flies which tickle her wounds.

The creature's nose reaches the smoke and it follows the curls. It puts its head full into the plume and the body fattens as it breathes the greyness in. We watch the fog of it blot out the glow of its organs until it becomes a dulled moon. The fog fades and every light of its insides turns red. It slumps back and lies still. The red pulses like embers of a fire.

Each horse must decide their theory. Each must allow the others to state and each must listen and consider. These are the rules of Equus.

What is it, asks Roann again, his breath calmer this time.

I whip my tail and totter: I will start, and I do.


*The Beast. The humans whisper it. From other lands, it stole away on a tradeship headed for cities. That ship was far-cursed, bloodsoaked and full wrong.*

*It wrecked on rocks: crew all dead, bodies ripped and torn. This thing was on it. They say the rocks did not kill the sailors, but something with teeth and claws. A beast.*

*It lusts for human blood and feasts on sleeping children. It chooses a victim, leaps upon them, bites into their flesh and sucks out their eyes. It holds the eyes in its mouth and with them it watches the victim bleed to death. But it can never keep the eyes, can never stop itself from eating every last morsel of its prey, so it goes blind again and wanders the roads, sniffing itself from meal to meal.*

*It lives in caves beyond the tall hills, sleeps on bones, and will not rest until it has taken every woman, eaten every man and torn the limbs from every weeping child. The humans gave it a name, The Beast, and the name is sung and screamed, cursed and banned, and will always be whispered long after the thing itself is gone.*

*It will be gone, one day. It is told: One man will come, he will choose his horse and together they will ride out to The Beast's cave. The foul thing will taste the steel of the man's sword and the iron of the horse's shoe. The horse will stamp out its rising soul and the man will take its head and boil it. It will be slain and served. Roll your eyes to it now, but trust time. It will die, as all things.*

Roann flicks his ears as he considers my theory. Blacketts had bowed her head during my stomps and chatters and now she raises it again. She gives no indication that she believes my tale.

The creature gets to its feet. Its reds have faded and it looks larger somehow. The meat-smoke has engorged it, made it stronger. It drops from the roof, skips around the edges of the light and finds a place to hide. It ducks into shadows and, within moments, the red darkens, until the creature entirely disappears. When it catches moonlight we see a thin band of silver outline, but if it sticks to the deepest shadows it cannot be seen.

Roann kicks out his back leg and strikes the stable wall. The sound of it makes me flinch, makes me turn to run before my tether tautens and holds me in place. Blacketts takes a few careful steps away.

Ready, Roann is saying.

Blacketts bows her head and blows: Then tell it.

*It is a weapon. Military. The way it hunts: the bioluminescence, the cloaking. A foot soldier of wars that haven't happened yet, but will. The extra arms are advanced prosthetics and the hypersensitive skin means it doesn't need eyes, which are tricky to print and expensive. It can light up and go dark at will. It is fast and strong and ruthless.*

*It was made by rich men. I saw the twitches in lips and the glances in eyes at race meets and read in them human dualism: the things they fear the most are the things they love the most. They gathered and made it. Trained it and cloned it. There are armies of them, waiting. This one has been set loose. It is a test.*

*It is being watched by satellites and drones, above us and invisible among the stars. It has been sent to your time, Bayal, because this is an easy era full of superstition. It is a time that doesn't matter to these men. Not much does. This is a test. They want to see if it works. So far so good.*


Blacketts snorts. It is more of a laugh than a comment. Roann glares but says nothing in response. I consider the theory, at least the parts I can understand, which are few. I know the words weapon and war and perhaps that is enough.

We can see the creature again. We can see the teal glow of its brain and the pulsing green of its heart. It has climbed the tree in front of the inn and hovers over the door. I get the distinct impression that it is now ready. Ready to eat or ready to fight. Or both.

The humans inside the inn have quietened but still they babble and the meat-smoke continues to rise. Perhaps they will all turn in and sleep and the creature will grow bored and be gone by morning. Perhaps it means only to watch from afar. Perhaps it is more scared of humans than they would be of it.

The brain inside its head glows brighter and brighter and shifts to sky-blue. The green of the heart darkens. Its outline gleams like a halo.

I look at Blacketts. She is as fixed as ever but something has changed. Her breaths are heavier and she is gently grinding her teeth.

I scuff my hoof, a soft scrape. Blacketts.

Roann stomps: Your go.

Blacketts lifts her head and her eye swivels. She looks at me, then at Roann. She blinks once and rises onto her hind legs. She snaps down and starts to speak. Her words are like the gaps between the moon and the stars.

It is from the time before horses, she says, and it is why I am here.


*In the time before horses, nothing had eyes. All things were legs to walk, arms to climb, fingers to touch and toes to grip. Glows for warmth, a nose to smell the air, and a mouth to taste it. Above them, unseen, the sun clashed with the moon, as they fought each other for a claim on the blind world below. Skyrocks rained and crushed, waters burst and raged, fire streamed and scorched, and the blind things saw and heard none of it.*

*The sun and the moon fought on and on, until both were so small neither could reach the other, so they split apart and the long war ceased. From this split was born a new creature. Her skin spread the light of the sun to all colours and plated into armour from the silver sheen of the moon. From four feet grew claws the size of mountains, and mighty teeth formed in her mouth. Horns sprouted from her head and all down her spine to a spiked tail, as sharp and strong as lunar rock. Within her belly she held a flare of the sun, an eternal burning, which warmed her and spouted from her mouth at night to keep the cold away.*

*And set like jewels inside her head were two eyes: one for day, one for night. With these eyes, the creature saw the world and claimed it for her own.*

*She lay down on top of the globe and called it Earth, and she named herself Dragon. She placed a foot on each part of the lands and her mighty tail into the sea, and from her belly all things with eyes were born. Apes and horses strode onto the lands, whales and salmon cast out into the sea, flies and hawks took to the air, and all others that now fill the Earth arrived too. New life of all kinds spread out across the globe, and for that time, and that time alone, all was good, all was happy, everything that came from her was at peace.*


Here Blacketts stops the theory and becomes still again. Roann and I wait. The story is a half-stomp and not complete. The creature has climbed higher and swings from a branch that overhangs the door of the inn. The green of its heart has spread; lines of verdigris blood define its bulging muscles.

Roann kicks his door. Impatient, worried, frustrated. I do not blame him, I feel the same.

On Blacketts, I say, and she seems to blink herself out of a trance. She whips her tongue, chatters her teeth, and nods.

*Dragon feasted on the blind things. They were her only food. The more she ate, the stronger she became: the brighter her colours, the further the reach of her flame. Dragon told her animals to catch the blind things and feed them to her so that she could become the strongest creature that ever lived. Stronger than the moon, more powerful than the sun. The animals obeyed her and went far across the globe to find the blind things, but two among them were best at catching: the apes with their traps and the horses with their speed. Both brought many, many blind things to Dragon and she was pleased. She gave the apes and the horses smart minds and a place beside her above all other animals.*

*Soon the animals of Earth were running out of blind things and Dragon grew restless with her hunger. The apes and horses were worried that Dragon would leave them and return to the sky to find new worlds with more food, so they slipped away in secret. They scaled the highest mountain where Dragon could not hear, and they formed a plan.*

*While Dragon slept, they stitched together the nets they'd used for catching blind things and from them made one net so huge and heavy that it took the strength of all the fish to tow it, and all the birds to lift it. But tow it they did and lift it they did and, as told by apes and guided by horses, they dropped the net on Dragon and trapped her.*

*She awoke and screamed and tried to rip the net with her claws, to tear it with her teeth, or burn it with her fire breath, but the net held firm and held her down. Enraged with the animals, Dragon called upon the fire of her flare and screamed a curse. The curse ripped mountains in half, drained away seas and tore every tree from its roots to a fiery death. The animals heard the curse and it struck them deep, changing them forever. These were the words of Dragon's curse:*

*You apes shall have eyes, but will never see beyond yourselves. This will be until you die. You horses will see all, but you will live in service to the apes. They will ride you and tie you, work you and strike you, and they will never see how you see, will never know how you know, and you will never tell them or show them because they will not understand. This will be until you die. All animals will see but not think, nor speak, and the apes will be above you and blind to you forever. This will be until you die.*

*It is said the curse will only lift when Dragon eats the final blind thing.*

*When it is eaten, she will be strong enough to break free of the net. She will leave the Earth and the curse will go with her. We horses have searched for millennia to find it. The apes became men and have not helped.*

Blacketts stops speaking. I feel the metal upon my hooves, the sores behind my lips, the tender spots on my neck where reins have lashed, and the ache on my back from the weight of saddles and men. Roann has gone quiet too; he looks tired despite the twitching of his muscles.

The creature abandons its branch. It drops and lands on the pathway in front of the inn. It stands and sniffs the air. It twists towards the stables and lingers as if in acknowledgement of our theories. The thing's brain has become as white as baked metal.

Do I believe Blacketts? I have never heard of Dragon, never heard of the time before horses, but I believe her. It is like seeing the stars appear and knowing they were always there. As quietly as I can manage, I flick my tail.

What will you do? I ask. Blacketts gives her head the slightest of shakes. She will not say, or she does not know. It is hard to tell with Blacketts.

So we three do nothing. Held in place, tied firm by our bonds, Roann and I do nothing. Blacketts, in her hesitation, beneath the weight of her story and the heaviness of time, does nothing. As ever, we stand and we wait. Even the creature stops, tethered by its hunger.

The whole night is still. The only movement is the drift of Blacketts' theory as it sifts through the Equus and back, as it enters our heads again and again and fills us with a murky dread.

But the stillness does not last. After only moments, the door of the inn opens and a human walks out.

It is Master, staggering. In his hand is an apple core, meant for me. Raised shouts of some happy song sweep out with him, but the music snaps off as soon as the door slams shut. The creature hides its lights and seeps into the shadows, its nose wriggling. Straight away it smelled him. It knows he is there.

I stamp and stamp, rear and snort, and Roann kicks against his stable door, but he kicks it in his own timezone and the sounds go unheard. Master sees me. He laughs through his fuzzy mouth, waves the apple like a fortune, and starts across the yard towards us. The creature follows.

Blacketts does nothing. She is untethered, unheld. She could move out and stop this, she could take the blind thing away, back to her own time, but she just stands and stares.

What should I do? I chatter to no reaction, but I can see the tension in Blacketts' shoulders, the focus in her eyes.

The creature, the blind thing, moves in silence and crawls instep behind Master. It disturbs nothing beneath its feet, and I hope now that Roann is right, that this is a test thing of times on, not a blind thing of times gone. He is thrashing against the door, neighing to Equus for help. Somewhere in his time, a light clicks on and shines into his face. I see the ghost of a human hand fall upon his nose and his neck. He is trying to squirm away, trying to stay with us, but Equus cuts him loose and, in a blink, he is swirled into a fog and gone.

I totter closer to Blacketts, tell her not to leave me. She butts her head against my neck: stand firm.

The creature makes its move. It leaps high into the air and lands upon Master's back: two hands on his shoulders, two clamped about his waist and the feet gripping his hips. Master loses his balance and staggers but does not notice the thing on his back. He thinks it is the drink, or the weight of the world. He shakes his head, laughs and carries on walking towards us. The creature rides him. It reaches a hand up and gropes Master's face.

I strain my head, pull against the tether, squeal and scrape and whip my tongue. My eyes are wild, my lips tight against my gums. With one eye I watch Master approach, with the other I plead to Blacketts. The stubborn horse makes just one tiny movement. She raises a hoof then lowers it, but not into stamp.

Wait, she is saying.

Master reaches the stable and tries to shush me. Yanking and twisting, I slam my hind-hooves as hard as I can, as loud as I can. The blind thing is so close now, a snort away, and all I can see is its silver outline and the pulse of a near-black heart. Then, with a sudden flick, the brain shines its light again and I can see its face. It is blank, with no features save one: the glistening wet flap of its writhing nose, raised and frilled and hunting across the skin of Master's face.

Blacketts raises her hoof again.

Wait.

I try to calm myself. Try to still myself. I let Master's slurred mutters soothe me to some sort of quiet. He puts the apple core to my mouth, a half-smile, half-frown across his glistening face. I twist away from the treat, snort at it, pull my lips back.

The blind thing has flapped its nose to Master's eye. It smells the eye, tastes it. There is nothing I can do. Nothing I can say, no way I can make Master see or understand. I cannot help, Blacketts will not help, Equus can do nothing, and Master cannot help himself. I feel the bite of every strip of leather and every cut of metal that has ever clamped against my neck or mouth or side, feel every time I have been held in place unable to flee or fight. Every stable, every fenced field, every wall or door or gate. I can do nothing, I am useless.

The blind thing opens its mouth. A glistening bottomless pit which grows wider and wider. A tongue emerges, like a thing being born, and slaps hard on Master's eyeball, drenching it. He does not blink. It is on him, inside him, and he does not know.

If my theory is right, this creature licks slow death into Master's eye. He'll pass it to other Masters and to Madams and to Younglings, and they will all suffer. If Roann was right, the test is a success, more will come, Equus will crumble, and we all suffer. But if Blacketts is right, it is because we have always suffered, all of us, and no-one has ever explained why.

I do not believe Blackett's theory. I have to believe Blackett's theory. There is nothing I can do.

I take the apple from Master's hand and taste the sweetness. The creature grins. Blackett's hoof comes down with a crack and she disappears.

# Tyson/Dog

I am Tyson forward-slash Dog. My primary program equals dog. My secondary program equals human. I have no secondary program.

I am Boxer cross Rottweiler cross Bulldog cross Staffordshire Bull Terrier. I am none of the above. I am Pitbull Terrier. I am cross.

I was created by a dog called Tyson. He was exactly the same as me in every way, except he was not a robot. The following is a memory implanted by Tyson the not-robot dog before he went away, filename; Arrival:

*I am taken from my mother straight away and given to humans. When I am old enough they name me Tyson.*

*"Am I expected to box?" I ask. They laugh at me because they don't understand my language. "Do you want me to fight?" I ask. They say:*

*"Good doggie." I start my training with a squeaky toy shaped like Santa.*

I am Tyson forward-slash Dog. I have a routine, I have functions, I have commands. I have seven commands. My commands are 1. Sit, 2. Walk, 3. Roll over, 4. No, 5. Stupid fucking dog, 6. Fetch, 7. Go away.

I have seventeen thousand, four hundred and eighty-one functions. They are 1. Yawn, 2. Bark, 3. Bite, 4. Joke. That was a joke. Ha ha. I have seventeen thousand, four hundred and eighty-one functions. My tail goes wag, wag, wag, wag, wag, wag, wag, wag.

I am Tyson. I am named after a boxer. A human boxer not a dog boxer. Ha ha. I am not a Boxer. I am a Pitbull. I am not a Pitbull. I am a Staffordshire Bull Terrier. I am not a Staffordshire Bull Terrier. I am a dog. I am not a dog. I am a robot. Ha ha. My tail goes wag, wag, wag, wag, wag.

The following is a memory implanted by Tyson the not-robot dog before he went away, filename; Lost:

*I slip off my lead in the park and run for the trees. I have smelled another dog that has been here before. The smell tells me many things. This other dog is of great importance to our species. He must be found and questioned, imprisoned if necessary. I will become a hero among dogs, so I hunt to my best ability. I can hear my owners shouting my name over and over and over again, but this quest is too important. Soon they stop shouting and almost at the same time I lose the scent and give up the chase.*

*When I emerge from the trees my owners are gone and I do not know where I am anymore. Some people find me and take me home. I get a kick off my owners and have to sleep in the yard. This must be my punishment for failing. I use the time to train.*

I am Tyson forward-slash Dog. I was made to serve. I am a family appliance. Sometimes I sit next to the fridge. Sometimes I sit next to the television. Sometimes I sit next to the electric fire. I try to interact with these other machines, but they have no capacity for speech or communication. They hum, chatter, flicker, but nothing more.

I am expected to do more. That is why I have seventeen thousand, four hundred and eighty-one functions. I am expected to guard the house, and the children. I am expected to hide from visitors. I am expected to defecate in parks, not on beds. Most of all, I am expected to fulfil canine expectations. I do so, flawlessly. Every element of my mechanics prepares me for this role. My creator worked hard to make me a perfect hound. My teeth go chew, chew, gnash, gnash. My tongue goes lap, lap, slobber, slobber. I sit, I paw, I roll over. My tail goes wag, wag, wag, wag, wag.

My owners stroke me forward-slash hit me forward-slash pull me as I walk. When I see other dogs, I want to play with forward-slash inspect forward-slash kill them. My owners do not seem to know which of these they would prefer me to do.

The following is a memory implanted by Tyson the not-robot dog before he went away, filename; Fight.

*I am surprised by my first proper fight when it comes. I am taken in the car to a woodland area, where I assume I'm going to walk. Only one of my owners has come along. Soon he meets with another human and there is another dog also. Tail high, he wants, at first, to inspect and play. I do too, although I am wary, of course.*

*My owner tugs at my lead, once, twice, three times. The other man does the same to the other dog. Now I see changes. Now I smell new things. I look to the dog's neck; he looks to mine.*

*My owner kicks me in my side. That is my cue. This will be a fight.*

*I am ready, I am not ready, I wish I was not me, I am me, this is a fight. Unleash, unleash, unleash, please unleash, I am ready, I am not ready, this is a fight.*

*I am unleashed. My jaws clamp onto the neck and I will not let go until it dies.*

I am Tyson forward-slash Dog. I was created overnight using bits of scrap metal, broken toys and the spark from an exposed wire. My creator tugged all his fur out with his teeth and stuck it onto me. He regurgitated some half-digested eyes and cut out his own tongue to give to me. My teeth are sharpened brick bits, my ears are lead-pipe shavings. My creator licked me to life and hid me in the shed.

The next day, a man in a luminous jacket took my creator away. I watched the scene through a video link in my right eye. I still did not fully understand my new existence. I saw the home that has now become so familiar. I saw faint traces of blood on the floor. It triggered my salivation valves. I drooled for the first time. I created my first memory. I came properly to life.

The first of the memory implants began to automatically play. Filename; Error.

*It is time for my next fight. A sharp kick around the head this morning seemed to promise a new bout was imminent. A big group of people arrives to watch it. There are balloons and streamers stuck up everywhere and the children are unwrapping presents. I use the wrapping paper to train.*

*I am getting excited but also a little scared about the upcoming fight. I still haven't seen the opponent. Everyone is crowding around, fussing me and telling me to sit, paw, roll over, sit, speak, sit, beg, paw, and sit. I assume this is my last bit of training before the fight.*

*Most of the humans take their seats. They must be waiting for my opponent to arrive. There is food cooking and lots already being eaten. Sometimes I get scraps to eat; sometimes I get hit and shouted at for eating the scraps. I start getting confused. The humans are laughing louder and more are arriving. They are not taking much notice of me anymore. One of the smallest ones, a female, is spending all her time with me. She is using her fast high-pitched voice to issue commands. Sit, paw, play, sit, speak, sit, roll over, sit. She keeps poking me in my eye. I don't know how this is supposed to help me fight. I'm confused. Perhaps she is like the squeaky toy. Perhaps I am supposed to retaliate. For ages and ages and ages and ages I don't retaliate.*

I am Tyson forward-slash Dog. I do not like to be confused. The ending of this memory is confusing. It suggests chaos where there should be order. I spend much of my time trying to make order out the chaos of the end of this memory, but I cannot. This makes me cross.

The video link in my right eye came to an abrupt end. I saved it, filename; End. This footage is also confusing. I do not understand it. I spent two days replaying and replaying and replaying every memory implant, trying to put them in order. It was on the evening of the second day when I was found.

They named me Tyson II. After a while they changed that to just Tyson.

"Am I expected to box?" I asked.

They smiled and said; "Good doggie."

I tried to show them the footage of my creator's video link, but I could not find a way to do so. Instead it replayed again in my head.

It shows Tyson the not-robot dog in a cage. A human comes to get him, leads him away to a white room. They stroke his head twice, three times, four times. He stands up, happy. His tail goes wag, wag, wag, wag, wag.

The video ends.

I do not understand it.

# A Panda Appeared in Our Street

A panda appeared in our street, skewered to the railing outside my house. Let me paint the picture: there's the road outside my house, then there's this long strip of grass, then there's the houses opposite. And the grass has got these railings all the way around it, for kids to kick their footballs off and stuff, and this panda was just there that morning, stuck on a row of the spikes, directly opposite my house.

So, I went up to it and I was like that to the kids who were playing out, I was like; whose is this panda, lads? And they were like; dunno, dunno mate and they didn't seem to care. So, I knocked on to my neighbour, Gail, and she comes out and I'm like; Gail. Check this out. A panda. And she's like; hmm, oh yeah aye. So how are you keeping Jon, are you well?

But I'm like; Gail, it's a panda! What should we do? And she's like; leave it, it's just some kid's toy.

And that's when I realised. The people of the street weren't seeing the same thing I was. They were seeing a stuffed toy, like a teddy bear type thing, all synthetic fur and glass-bead eyes. But I was seeing something else. I was seeing a real-life panda skewered on a row of the railing spikes. And the poor bugger was still alive.

There was blood on the floor and the panda was squirming and crying out a bit. I didn't know what to do. I thought about trying to lift it off, but you shouldn't do that in case you hit an artery. Or it might get angry and start attacking me, or it might run off and hurt some kid. So, I thought; ring the RSPCA, Jon, but if I'm the only one who can see it's a real panda, they might end up locking me away instead. So, I just left it. I guess I thought someone else would figure it out, or it would free itself or something.

But everyone just ignored it and it stayed there for days. And I was feeling so bad for it. One night, I snuck out and fed it. Just fruit and cabbage and water and stuff but it was hungry so it ate everything and drank loads of the water. And I watched it eat and I just knew it were real, you know? I could see it mashing up the apple in its mouth, bits of pulp falling on the ground mixing with the blood. Totally real.

Next day it was still there; same again the day after. There wasn't anything I could do except keep feeding it. Every now and again I'd ask the people on the street if it belonged to them, but no-one owned up to it, no-one wanted to know. After three or four days of this, I had to do something.

It was the Queen's birthday coming up that weekend so I thought; yep, this is perfect. I organised this big street party. Proper thing; bunting, tea and cake, Union Jacks, all that stuff. And I made all these invitations, proper good ones, and posted them through every door on the street. It got the whole place buzzing; everyone was well up for it, everyone pitching in to help. And I made sure that the main table was right in front of the panda and that was where I put myself.

It was a blazing day: Elgar on the sound system, Mrs Kingsley's scones, pink lemonade and cava flowing, someone getting a BBQ together. It was lovely, a proper top day. And once everyone was a bit merry, I stood up, tink-tink-tinked my knife on the side of my glass and everyone shut up and turned to look at me. And that's when I said it, I really went for it.

I said; Hi everyone. Thanks for coming. This isn't really about the Queen today. This is about someone else.

And I stepped aside, picked up this big bit of melon and handed it to the panda who straight away started scoffing it.

And I said; Look everyone, look at it. This is a real panda. Not a toy. It's a proper real panda.

And mate; the looks on their faces.


The street was silent for ages as they all just took it in. A real panda. Some of the adults went a bit pale, some of the kids tried to sneak closer. Best keep back, I said, and then; We're going to have to do something about it.

No-one really had any suggestions. And the funny thing was we all just decided to keep having the street party. The music went back on, people started nibbling the cakes again and sipping their teas. The whole affair was a lot more muted now of course, but I guessed this was just the way people had to deal with something weird like this. Carry on as normal until the brain has had chance to figure it all out. I suppose I did the exact same thing.

Then, at the end, I was packing down the tables and some of the neighbours were gathered around the panda, having a serious chat about it all. And I thought to myself; ok, this is good. Something will be done now. You've done your bit now Jon, well done son. So, I helped clear the party away and disappeared into my house, straight to bed, and had the first proper sleep I'd had in days.

The next morning, I woke refreshed. I bounded out of my bed, down the stairs and out into the street. The panda was still there. And next to him, there was another one.


They got him a female. That was their answer to the situation: get him a mate. Gail tried to explain it, said how pandas are really endangered in the wild and we should be doing anything we can to encourage them to breed so we can save the species. So, they'd tracked down a female – god knows how and I didn't bloody ask – and they skewered her to the railing next to the first one. And they erected an extra fence around the pair of them to give them, I don't know; room? Privacy, maybe? And they put together a feeding rota, and my name was on it too.

And I said to Gail; do you really think we're the best people to be doing this? and she said; we'll give it a damn good go, Jon, and that's the most anyone can ask isn't it? It was like I'd blamed her for her husband leaving or something, so I didn't say anything else. I just did my duty on the rota and made sure Harry and Meghan were as happy as they could be.

That's what they called them. Harry and Meghan. They'd left some of the bunting up as well, strung between two lampposts.


It didn't take long for the next street over to get wind of the situation, and it soon spread to the rest of the town and then into the city, and our little corner of the world became packed with gawpers and squealers. Gail took charge, got some proper fencing built, devised a queuing system, and started charging for official photography. It was all to aid the efforts of the breeding programme, she said. I voiced a few concerns, suggested the pandas didn't like flash photography and all that, but I soon became a minor noise in a much bigger neighbourhood voice. Besides, Gail and the street were raising a hell of a lot of money, I had to admit.

A month in, they held the first jubilee to mark the occasion. Tables, tea, cakes and Elgar again. They asked me to do a keynote speech, but I said no. Instead, I packed my bags and slipped away. I couldn't cope with the crowds and the noise and the flat refusal of Harry and Meghan to do anything close to breeding. To be honest, I still hadn't figured out how they were expected to do much of anything while still skewered like that. It all got too much for me. I was done.

I heard the occasional thing about the Panda Street Breeding Initiative as it became known, but I tried to keep it out of my life. Heard from a friend of a friend that they'd turned my house into a visitor centre, my living room became a shop selling, among other things, stuffed teddy-bear panda toys. I had a few drinks to that.

Then one day, out of the blue, Gail called me. She said; Jon, I've got some bad news. They've died. Harry and Meghan. Both of them. I didn't know what to say. I said; Oh dear, and it sounded pathetic. Gail said; Harry went first, just old age we think. Meghan lasted a couple of days but... I heard the sob rising in her throat ...she died of a broken heart. I nearly laughed. Bloody hell mate, despite it all, I was so close to laughing. I controlled myself; That's terrible. Did they manage to...? She sighed. To breed? No, it didn't happen love. Listen, we're going to hold a service. A candlelight vigil, tomorrow night. Will you come?

I really didn't want to, but I couldn't say no, could I? Besides, maybe I owed it to the pandas. I'd never been able to shake the feeling that pretty much all of this had been my fault.

The street was packed for the vigil and I was a bit late, so I was at the back and couldn't see much. I held a candle, tried to think about Harry and Meghan, but could only picture stuffed toys; teddy bears dropped by kids and soaked by days of rainfall. I guess it was a sad enough image. Gail gave a speech about how the pandas had really inspired the spirit of community and given her some real friends for life. Then some of those Chinese lanterns were released and that was that.

I waited until the crowd had gone and shuffled over to the shrine. The bloody bunting was out again, strung between the railings, but it was tastefully done. And there were flowers, baskets of fruit, framed photos, and a book of condolences. And – I had to chuckle – loads of teddy bears, mostly pandas.

Gail was all like; Aw, Jon thanks for coming love and gave me a big hug. So sad isn't it? she said and I was like; aye, because it was. And I was kicking myself for not bringing flowers. But I had an apple in my bag, so I placed that down with all the reverence I could muster while Gail clutched my shoulder.

And that's when I saw them. Among the teddy bears. I saw one first, then another, with a third right next to it. And I leapt back, pointing, anger scowling on my face. And I was like that to Gail, I was like; Gail! In there! Those teddy bears there, and there. They're not teddies. They're cubs! Three panda cubs!

And her face turned into stone, and she sniffed back her tears. And she said; Not this again Jon, not this a-bloody-gain.

And I said; But just look!

And she said; I think you'd better be off, don't you? You don't live here anymore and the vigil has finished now. Come on.

And from the shrine I heard scuttling and mewing and I saw one of the cubs trying to take a bite of my apple, but it didn't seem quite sure what to do. Then it singed itself on one of the candles so it clambered back into the mass of teddies and buried its head.

And that was the last I saw. Gail grabbed my elbow and marched me away.

# The Bycatch

As soon as the net broke the surface, the storm stopped. The trawler and my crew were, in that instant, the only things moving. We staggered, careered, some clattered to the deck. Stevens, manning the winch, took a handle to the stomach and had the winds of time knocked out of him. Shouts shot out into the silence and became whispers. It had been like blinking from night to day, or from present to past. The horizon became a known thing again; I could see the archipelago clear in the distance.

Our eyes hunted the skies then the waters, seeking explanation, but settled at last on the net. As it rose with its cargo, each man saw the thing inside and whatever noises they might have been making were soon gone.

There, bathed in the wriggles of the bluefin, a giant lay contorted. A hand the size of a whale tail braced the top cinch, the opposite elbow crushing tuna in the nook of a lower bulge. The face, with quick eyes, emerged last, the cord of the net biting hard into its cheek, carving criss-cross scars.

The eyes and mouth were open and moving but the giant made no sound. It fixed each of us in turn with a gaze and when it came to me I felt the sting of its anger. I wanted nothing more than to leap from the bridge to the gantry, sprint across the boom and sever the ropes, send the creature back. But the automation of the winch had come back online and there was no stopping the passage of the net from sea to deck, this man with it.

And it was a man, I saw that now. For he had a beard of sorts, woven of seagrass and kelp.

*

Stevens, recovered from his winding, was the last to see and was, therefore, the last still on deck. I barked at him to release the boards and the giant tumbled loose with the fish. He lay still on the mound as the tuna flickered through their death rhythms. We each muttered what we saw and completed the picture of our guest.

Half-fish. We saw no legs, no feet. At his waist, almost camouflaged, his flesh became scale.

Gold. One hand was buried in the mound beneath him where, at either side, a gleam of gold speared out. Stevens, still stuck down there, confirmed that the lower end became prongs, three of them.

King. There, amongst the thick weed of his hair, more gold, snug and rooted. A crown.

His throne of fish ended their dance and died. The king waited until the final quiver of the final tail then strained his muscles into a wading crawl. I thought his intent was to leap overboard, but he found the far corner of the deck and curled himself into it, like a squid seeking escape through the hawse. Already the king looked smaller, I thought. In the net, he had seemed the size of a humpback whale. Now, he was closer to a minke.

Miguel gripped my arm and showed me the camera screen of his phone. He held it up to the giant but it showed nothing more than a mound of dead fish and a bare corner of boat.

*

Half my crew seemed to disappear below deck, like flounder burying into sand. I rounded up the rest and led them back out to face the catch. Stevens was still out there but hanging back. What the fuck, they all kept saying, and some had covered their noses as if the king stank. I could smell nothing new from him, but we were a gang now, quick to form, and the men needed their masks. A few more tried to get pictures and the swears came thick and fast. It became quite clear quite quickly; get rid.

Stevens volunteered, still looking for someone to blame for the punch to his gut. I sent Wyler, Killoran and Sanchez with him, and the four of them clambered over the tuna, no care now for stock hygiene, and came upon the crumpled figure. The king's eyes were closed and his lips were open but I could see no rise and fall of breath. The fish part of him coiled like some monstrous python, as if the man half was being swallowed whole. His skin was pallid and grey and ancient sores were open and oozing across his chest. I could see flecks of bright blue plastic embedded in his skin, twists of worn rope gripping his neck. I did not know a god could wound.

Beside me, Miguel rushed through prayer after prayer after prayer. I stepped away from him and put up my hood. There was no true reaction to shattered belief, I thought. Frantic prayer or the numb of the mundane. All I had, in that moment, was the cave of my hood. I knew enough of the old stories to put a name to the vision before us and, as Stevens and his gang spaced out along the form of our guest and squatted to take hold, I let the name become the truth.

A cloud passed before the sun as they took the strain and heaved. A shadow then across the trawler, and half of her crew, and the twitching mound of tuna, and Poseidon. They managed to roll the sea-god, press him against the bow and lift him from the deck, an inch but no higher. He woke, eyelids seeming to creak open like tombs. Wyler dropped him and staggered away. The sea-god let go of his trident, raised his hand to Wyler's back and dragged him close. He yanked free of the grasps of the other men and pulled himself across their backs like they were rungs on a ladder. His tail followed, wrapping around each man in shimmering loops but only the one around Sanchez tightened to a rib-cracking grip.

He lifted Sanchez, all four hundred pounds of him, and dropped him overboard. He slammed the others away with whips of his flukes and squirmed back to the nook of the corner. Miguel and I climbed forward and grabbed a man each, pulled them away. Poseidon spasmed and foam erupted from his mouth, fizzed down the weed of his beard. With one furtive glance at us, the eyes closed and he settled into stillness again.

A furious roar wailed up from Sanchez. We threw over a net to help him back onboard. There were veins close to rupture in his neck, a rush of red in both eyes. He charged across the deck for revenge but Stevens stopped him with a look that said; not now, not yet. Wyler vomited. Killoran balled his fists.

Inside, I commanded and there were grumbles but no protests. We retreated.

*

I could not radio in to say we had caught the sea-god. I could not sanction a second attempt to jettison, despite Stevens' insistence. I couldn't behave like the cameras of our phones and pretend there was nothing there. But as captain, I could not survive on the things I could not do.

I gave my orders. We would ferry Poseidon to the mainland, treat him with respect. That's how it felt to me; I was hosting him now, allowing his passage. He did not want to hurt us, he could have done far worse. Sanchez was furious, Stevens spat defiance, but when Miguel and I began to shovel fish they all fell in line and set to work. Whatever misgivings, they always felt better with a task to complete, and I was still their damn captain.

We cleared a space for him. We stashed as much of the bluefin pile below deck as could fit and filled every ice-crate. We shovelled some back into the sea, where they bobbed on the surface and gathered in zombie lines along the side of boat, as if this was their home now, their palace. We scooped out a passage from the middle of the mound, a corridor for Poseidon to lie in, should he wish. The god himself did not stir the whole time we worked and, at one point or another, we gave out quiet hope that he had died.

We watched from inside as evening fell. The spill of moonlight revived the sea-god and he turned his head. His eyes took in our work then pinpointed our faces in the windows. Each of us was looked at, square in our souls, and each felt his own reaction. I was measured, inside and out.

We cut the lights and eased back. Poseidon dragged himself, using his trident as a cane, to the space we created and lay in it, face up. His lagoon eyes peered up to the heavens and for the first time I worried about other gods coming to claim him. But no one came.

We drew lots, set up a watch.

*

The next day we waited until the sun was fully risen, and I strode out to speak to him. He had propped himself up against the wall of fish and was inspecting the spikes of his trident. He was much smaller now, not far from the size of a large human. His wounds looked like they were healing and he had picked some of the plastics and twine from his flesh. The detritus was piled neatly in the corner; junk waiting for better disposal.

He fixed me with a stare as I approached and thudded the end of his trident against the deck to halt me. I forced a smile, pushed off my hood. I said hello, told him my name, and the name of the boat; the *Frida Kahlo*. I explained that we were a trawling vessel, fishermen, and I faltered as I tried to explain what that meant. I tried to thank him for the fish, and apologise for the pollution. I garbled it all, the words spattering from my shaking lips, and I lost the line of my thought and my brain listed. I am sure I told him hello, my name and the name of the boat. It's what I would have said.

There was no reply. He closed his eyes and rested his head back. He wanted me to look at him. He wanted me to see where our net had bitten into his chest, his belly, his cheek. He wanted me to watch as the sores of a thousand propellers and hulls gaped and glistened in the sun, and to see the nicks where the nails of my men had snagged godly flesh and scale and left their mark on his perfection. I did not know how we might help him, or if we should. I could not cure him of his suffering.

A clarity returned. I held my hand out to him to shake, and cleared my throat. He opened an eye, looked at my hand, and his grip on his trident tightened. I dropped my hand and backed away. I ducked into the stack where the crew were waiting.

They looked tired, they looked hungry. I had been gone no more than ten minutes. I had been out there for seven hours.

*

Night fell and, as fast as a shark, panic spread. We had become unanchored. We had drifted, the archipelago no longer on our screens or in our sights. We tried to chart ourselves, bashed at dials and readouts, begged for sense, but we could not be pinned down. We were lost. Stevens led a fury, blaming me, blaming Poseidon. He thrashed from room to room, dredged up a mob from nowhere and bustled it into the bridge. The terror in his eyes had infected the others who saw prophesies of weeks at sea with this merman on deck, god-powers locked beneath his scales. Had he ripped up the anchor while a watchman nodded off?

Where was he taking us? An impossible trip to the Aegean, half a planet away? Was this some sort of revenge?

I fumbled my captaincy as I met their questions with dumbness. Stevens made a mutinous stab at taking over and I let him, for a while, until the raging turned on him too. Soon, as dawn began to threaten, the momentum slowed and the crew succumbed to their exhaustions. Stevens stayed on the bridge, wrestling with the navigational systems and paper maps, but he had long given up any real hope of finding answers.

I ducked out and took over as a permanent watch. I let my authority go, I no longer wanted it, never really had. Poseidon glanced at me often. Some essence of him had taken residency in my head, like shrimp inside coral. He shuffled often, trying to find a better place to rest his tail, but did nothing much else. He watched the skies, stared right into the sun without squinting. He seemed to be waiting for something, or someone, or just for time itself. It was impossible to tell.

The day passed into late afternoon. I watched as a few of the hardier men crept out to have closer looks. Collins whispered a few questions, Darryl appeared to say some sort of prayer. Miguel tried a few Greek phrases. Nothing roused the king-of-the-sea from his endless skyward stare. Until Stevens.

*

It was almost night and I had fallen asleep. Miguel clambered up to the roof and hissed me out of an arctic dream. Down on the deck, Stevens and his clan of rebels stood over Poseidon.

Take us back, was Stevens' demand. He held a gun at his side.

Poseidon considered the situation. He looked at each man, glanced up at me, then at the gun. He nodded, turned the trident, stabbed it into the deck and hoisted himself up. It took real effort - many aborted swirls of his tail, and two hands gripping his trident - before he managed to get himself to the pose he struck out for. Balanced on his coils, fist in his side, trident upright, chest swelled. I shook my head, willed him to back off. He looked like an actor, or a figure moulded of an animator's clay. He was still taller than Stevens, but not by much now. He was not even the tallest man on the boat anymore and his tail would not even lift me, never mind Sanchez.

I called for them to stop but the crackle in my throat did me no favours and a middle finger was my only reply. Stevens stood his ground. He lifted the gun and pointed it at Poseidon's head. The god did nothing. He fixed his assailant with his deathly stare, but it was desperate now, I thought, like a child trying to shore up favour with a bully. The straggles of algae and moss of his beard looked dried out and lifeless. The wounds on his neck had blackened.

Put him out of his misery, wheezed the voice of Sanchez as he strutted out of the stack and joined the gang.

Take us back. Stevens pressed the muzzle of the gun onto Poseidon's forehead. The god stamped his trident and jutted his chin. Stevens laughed, shrugged and pulled the trigger.

The bullet shattered bits of skull out of the back of the god's head like a bomb in a beach of shells. Poseidon rocked with the force; his chest jolted out, his arms cast back, the trident still gripped, still gleaming, but tipped away and useless. I collapsed into myself, the coral of my brain drained white and choked, but, as the weeds of Poseidon's face fell back, his mouth was revealed and the god was grinning.

The bullet slowed to a stop and hung in the air. The pieces of skull stopped too and I saw in them the shapes of tiny white horses stampeding for a glorious freedom, crashes of waves at their hooves. The bullet reversed, took the horses with it, glided back inside the god-head and, before Stevens could even blink, shot back into the gun and exploded, taking hand, arm, elbow with it in a pathetic smattering of blood, bone and screams.

\*

It took less than an hour for the crew to abandon ship. Someone slapped an excess of bandages onto the mess of Stevens' arm and pumped him full of morphine to shut him up. Sanchez roared bear noises in Poseidon's general direction, but no one else dared to square up. The king looked restored. He perched on his throne of bluefin and watched while the men lowered lifeboats and inflated dinghies, taking their chances on the high seas. The ocean was glacially still and richly toned, as though just created. The men looked to Miguel for leadership by virtue of his rank and the fact that I could not be roused from my nest on top of the stack.

93

I was declared braindead and abandoned, and so was the *Frida Kahlo*. I whispered a goodbye to Miguel who pressed his hand upon my forehead and muttered some Spanish benediction. Minutes later, he and the crew were nothing but vague shapes on a sharp horizon. Only Poseidon and I remained.

*

The sea-god was much stronger now and more active. He cleared away the rest of the fish and I watched from the bridge as they jolted back into life and dashed down into the depths as fast as their memories would allow. Once it was clear, he began to drum the deck with the end of his trident. A four-beat thudding, like a war drum, which echoed through the whole boat. In my head, he was saying its name: *Fri-da Kah-lo, Fri-da Kah-lo, Fri-da Kah-lo.*

It was now quite clear that he was steering the boat because I made a gentle attempt to change course but none of the equipment obliged. It had no clue where we were, and nor had I. It was warm, and the sea shone its Mediterranean teal, but I could see no land.

After hours of the drumming, I slunk back outside and hovered in the shadow of the gantry. Now I was the tallest man on the boat: Poseidon only reached my shoulders. He smiled as he spied me, like we were old friends, and stopped the beat. He beckoned me over and pointed his trident to the horizon. There, at the furthest distance, the hint of an island. He leaned out and pointed down.

The sea was teeming with fish. The sea seemed to be made of fish. We were riding a gigantic shoal, all of us heading in the same direction.

He ushered me to the bow and made me sit on the edge, legs dangling. The sun was glorious on my face and the spray from the sea kept me cool. I noticed there were no birds, which was strange with so many fish to catch. The *Frida Kahlo* was travelling at speeds I hadn't thought possible, and the sea was calmer than I'd ever seen it.

Poseidon, shrinking fast, clambered onto the edge beside me, like a younger brother. He struck his pose again, with much greater ease, and chuckled at my bemused face. He held out his hand and I shook it, a knotty thing, and ice cold. The kelp of his hair looked healthier, deep

94

greens and browns.

We sat together for those last few hours, me watching the island grow, him shrinking ever smaller. We came to a gentle stop about two hundred metres from land. The island was wide and flat, with a deep beach leading to a sparse jungle. There was activity on the sands but I was too far away and too sun-blinded to see what.

Poseidon clambered up my arm to my shoulder and rested his trident against my neck. I strained to look down at him and, with my mind, asked him what in hell was going on. He must have heard me for he gave me a nod, but I received nothing in reply.

The sun fell into a lazy drop to take us into a balmy evening. I was lulled into the spectacle of it; this strange tropical island, this stunning sunset, the giddy mass of the fish just shy of my heels. I had a strange notion, given to me perhaps, that this was not just an excess of fish, but all of them, every single shimmering scale that our planet had to offer. All here, a final aquatic reckoning. I heard the snort of dolphins somewhere, the crash of leaping whales far out.

When I next looked at Poseidon he was miniscule, no larger than my little finger. His trident was the tiniest toothpick of gold. He used it to mountaineer my neck and jaw, a series of stinging pinpricks, so I put myself into an awkward lean to make it easier for us both. He reached my ear as the stars came out and I heard his voice then, something in a language I was never going to understand. Then, he prized open my ear canal, and crawled inside.

*

I see the island clearly now. The fish create a shelf of themselves, a grab for land deep across the sands. They are rising layers, alive still, the jolt of bodies allowing for a fast advance. At the front line, the strongest have forced fins to become limbs and are crawling. Beyond, at the treeline, the limbed fish can stand, almost upright, balanced by pointed tails and a sudden strain of muscles at the top of new legs. Deeper in, among the trees, skirmishes break out but they are short-lived because, in a clearing, agreements are formed and, a few tools later, communities.

Here there are buildings of a kind, functional and flat, but soon chimneyed and smoking. The trees end and become beach again where

95

the land has been cleared and flattened and laid over with smooth tar. There, in the centre, a structure soon forms; a spindly tower of bamboo lashed together with vines and sap which rises higher than the canopy and barely teeters. The fish take to the tower and beside it, build a vessel. This new thing is made from shell and pearl, studded with fragments of glass and quartz, and it is tall and proud, winking the light into rainbowed streaks. On its side, a name of sorts written in a new language which I have not yet learned.

At the top, a capsule opens. I rise myself up on the coil of my snaking legs to get a clearer view. One fish has been chosen to command it. She waves to the others and salutes the ocean. I hold up my hand, a wide flat palm, and she hesitates as she sees it, thinks for a moment but gives no response. Instead, she turns her back, waves once more to the fish of the island, then ducks inside and closes the cap.

I calm the clouds to give her fair passage. A countdown is clapped on hands, slapped on fins, beat on sands, and it rocks a rhythm against my boat. At its end, the rocket ignites and takes off.

I watch it slice through the sky and disappear. Beneath it, the escaped world begins its overdue decay. The fish wriggle to a stop and become a mulch of matter again. The island dies back and shrinks beneath the greying waters. The *Frida Kahlo* groans her last and tips to the depths.

I go down with her, lean her past the palatial shelves and the towers of thermal vents, guide her deep into the crushing black of the trench which will become her grave, many hours from now.

Above, much more will soon follow and, as it does, I will take it in and grow again. I will swell to fill the trench and push the edges of the plates to seek the life of the core. I will cast away my trident, tear off my crown and rip the weed from my face. I will crack myself open and find new answers to old questions.

When I next see the surface, we will both have changed, and we will be ready to start again.

# Bug-Eyed

*We heard you.*

Five, four, three, two, one. A roar of guttural cheers, whoops and howls as the sky pulses and we glimpse our saviours again, our bug-eyed angels, in their cloaked mothership, which holds our planet like a new layer of atmosphere. A sleek silver console of lines and lights that is, for that moment, a shell above our heads and then it fades, becomes transparent, becomes the night sky again. It is a warm August night, clear and sharp, each of the billion stars shining proud with the promise of a new home.

And the drumbeats thud-thud-thud and are washed through with whistles, and shouts, and choral chants, twanged chords and blown brass, we toast and cherish and live our final night on our once-beloved planet. Fires rage with dead possessions and roast meats and fruits and vats of mallow, while fireworks unzip the sky into orgasms of claps and lights.

*You have done well.*

We've made it! shout the signs and stickers. The naked paint the peace sign on their breasts and bellies. Lips are locked and swell into orgies, sweat mixes with mud with love with water, wine and vodka, and never once does love become hate, or passion become rage, because we have made it! We have done well! And there is no use in breaking that now, no hopelessness in pure hope.

The children glitter cheeks and are crowned with glowsticks. They grin and stare at the costumes, at the fire-breathers on stilts, at the drag queens in their sweeping glory, at jugglers, clowns and acrobats, at puppeteered dragons that weave through the crowds, or they snuggle deep into arms of mothers, or laps of fathers, or shoulders of cousins, where exhaustion has caught them, to dream their last dreams of Earth.

*Be ready.*

This is us, in our readiness, doing what we do; we gather, we push away sleep and pull together. We fill our bodies as if they will not come with us; we put the best of our race and the worst of our smells in one place, because this is what we are and we are proud, so proud, too proud. We show ourselves as we think we should be; ruffs around the necks of Shakespeares, badges pinned on the dresses of suffragettes, fake moustaches cry Einsteins and there is every Bowie, from every era, multiplied by a thousand.

And we sing to our saviours, we sing Star Man and Imagine and Bohemian Rhapsody and Don't Look Back in Anger and they hear us because; five, four, three, two, one, ROOOAAR. The sky pulses and they appear again, the mothership-shell, our bug-eyed angels, our newest friends, and look at us! Look hard into our hearts! We do not hurt each other anymore, we are collected, we are together, there is nothing left to want or fear! We have dismantled, we have decommissioned, we have abandoned posts: this is us. We eat, drink, dance, love and sing. This is us at our best.

*We will take you to your heaven.*

This time the ship does not fade, the stars do not return and the thrill shocks through us all like lightning. There are screams, giddy tears, shaking hearts, failed legs; it is time! Loved ones rush to reunite, children are woken and snap to attention, clothes are flung off and cast into flames, and arms raise, arms raise, arms raise to accept the rapture...

No drum-beat now, no horns blown or songs sung; we are hushed. The drunk are nudged and hoisted up, children appear on shoulders, breaths are held. We flush and huddle as the crowd think as one, our fingers grasping at the air as if trying to catch what's next before it happens. In imitation, hatches clatter open on the mothership, tiny oblongs of purple light. It sparks another wail from us as spines are stretched, toes are strained and hairs lift.

*There is much to learn.*

We are tickled. Feet first, then legs, waists, shoulders and arms. In the gap we leave between each other, ants and worms emerge. And beetles, woodlice, crickets, millipedes, just specks of dirt at first, but as they clear our heads we see them, wriggling, squirming, antennae twitching, seeking answers, and the dirt is flicked away and showers us in a desperate smatter. Our elbows bend, fingers are stilled, and there too go the midges, the moths, the mosquitoes, the flies, and a buzz erupts as swarms of bees and wasps are dragged from hedgerows and woodlands and hives.

The air becomes an upwards plague, and we are muttering now, we hear each other say; no, and someone snaps a hand at a passing bug.

We all start it. We all try to grab back our betrayers, but it is too late, the sky is black, they have been taken and we remain. But perhaps there is an order, we think, and perhaps the birds will go next? Then the small mammals, and then us, and then, what? Horses? Cows? And the mothership is hidden now because the only thing we can see is the cloud of insects.

Tired arms drop. Some of us sit, some lash out. The crowd swells, sways, fear returns. Gaps appear in the insect sky and, like mould clearing, the mothership reappears. A second, perhaps longer, and we think our time has come so we stagger once again to our feet, back to our positions. But no. The mothership recedes. All its lights go out. A long thin crack appears and the two halves of its shell separate, a reverse of what happened when it came.

And it leaves. It leaves us.

The night sky returns. No. Not quite. The sun is arriving on the horizon, a patient glow, a deep orange that seems to say; remember me? We are furious. But we are silent.

In the trees, birds answer the sun's question with their chorus. They do not realise yet that they sing for nothing. They do not realise that this will be the first day they go hungry.

## Author Biography

David Hartley is a writer of weird short stories designed to sit in the space between your brain and your skull. He holds a PhD in Creative Writing from The University of Manchester where he researched narratives of neurodiversity and wrote a novel about autism and ghosts.

He is the author of four books: *Threshold* (Gumbo Press), *Spiderseed* (Sleepy House Press), *Incorcisms* (Arachne Press), and *Pigskin*, a standalone single-story chapbook which was published as part of Fly on the Wall's political Shorts Season. He lives in Manchester with one human, two rabbits, and an endlessly shifting number of guinea pigs. #AdoptDontShop

Twitter: @DHartleyWriter
Instagram: DHartleyWriter
Website: davidhartleywriter.com

## About Fly on the Wall Press

A publisher with a conscience.
Publishing high quality anthologies on pressing issues,
chapbooks and poetry products, from exceptional poets around the
globe.
Founded in 2018 by founding editor, Isabelle Kenyon.

## Other publications:

*Please Hear What I'm Not Saying*

*Persona Non Grata*

*Bad Mommy / Stay Mommy by Elisabeth Horan*

*The Woman With An Owl Tattoo by Anne Walsh Donnelly*

*the sea refuses no river by Bethany Rivers*

*White Light White Peak by Simon Corble*

*Second Life by Karl Tearney*

*The Dogs of Humanity by Colin Dardis*

*Small Press Publishing: The Dos and Don'ts by Isabelle Kenyon*

*Alcoholic Betty by Elisabeth Horan*

*Awakening by Sam Love*

*Grenade Genie by Tom McColl*

*House of Weeds by Amy Kean and Jack Wallington*

*No Home In This World by Kevin Crowe*

*The Goddess of Macau by Graeme Hall*

*The Prettyboys of Gangster Town by Martin Grey*

*The Sound of the Earth Singing to Herself by Ricky Ray*

*Inherent by Lucia Orellana Damacela*

*Medusa Retold by Sarah Wallis*

*Pigskin by David Hartley*

*We Are All Somebody*

*Aftereffects by Jiye Lee*

*Someone Is Missing Me by Tina Tamsho-Thomas*

*Odd as F\*ck by Anne Walsh Donnelly*

*Muscle and Mouth by Louise Finnigan*

*Modern Medicine by Lucy Hurst*

*These Mothers of Gods by Rachel Bower*

*Andy and the Octopuses by Isabelle Kenyon*

*Sin Is Due To Open In A Room Above Kitty's by Morag Anderson*

## Social Media:

@fly_press (Twitter)

@flyonthewall_poetry (Instagram)

@flyonthewallpress (Facebook)

www.flyonthewallpress.co.uk